"I was not going to be slave to these feelings."

"And here we are."

So simply she spoke of Alex's failure. So simply she laid out the inevitable.

"I want you," he said. "You must understand, it is not easy."

"I know. It isn't easy for me either."

He didn't have to explain this dark, tortured thing that aided him. Of course he didn't. Because it was like that for Tinley too. There was nothing sweet or simple about it. Nothing misty or magical. This was not fated soul mates. It was deeper than that. A tortured attraction that existed to make a mockery of all that he was. To make a mockery of whatever power he thought he might possess.

Their desire was the wolf pack. Come to devour them both.

And he surrendered.

Alex lowered his head and kissed her.

Maisey Yates is a *New York Times* bestselling author of over one hundred romance novels. She has a coffee habit she has no interest in kicking and a slight Pinterest addiction. She lives with her husband and children in the Pacific Northwest. When Maisey isn't writing, she can be found singing in the grocery store, shopping for shoes online and probably not doing dishes. Check out her website, maiseyyates.com.

Books by Maisey Yates

Harlequin Presents

His Forbidden Pregnant Princess
Crowned for My Royal Baby

Brides of Innocence

The Spaniard's Untouched Bride
The Spaniard's Stolen Bride

Once Upon a Seduction...

The Prince's Captive Virgin
The Prince's Stolen Virgin
The Italian's Pregnant Prisoner
The Queen's Baby Scandal
Crowning His Convenient Princess

Visit the Author Profile page
at Harlequin.com for more titles.

Maisey Yates

HIS MAJESTY'S
FORBIDDEN TEMPTATION

HARLEQUIN
PRESENTS

Recycling programs
for this product may
not exist in your area.

ISBN-13: 978-1-335-14907-7

His Majesty's Forbidden Temptation

Copyright © 2020 by Maisey Yates

This edition published by arrangement with Harlequin Books S.A.

For questions and comments about the quality of this book,
please contact us at CustomerService@Harlequin.com.

Harlequin Enterprises ULC
22 Adelaide St. West, 40th Floor
Toronto, Ontario M5H 4E3, Canada
www.Harlequin.com

Printed in U.S.A.

HIS MAJESTY'S
FORBIDDEN TEMPTATION

CHAPTER ONE

"WELL, I THINK the paperwork speaks for itself. Marriage is the only course of action."

Alexius de Prospero, Lion of the Dark Wood, Hope of the People, King of Liri, looked across from him at the small, plain woman. He was standing, which made her quite literally beneath him. She was sitting in a floral, overstuffed armchair looking frizzy and distressed.

In fairness, he had never seen Tinley Markham looking anything other than frizzy. It was hoped, on the day when the engagement had first been arranged between her and Alex's younger brother, that she would have been tamed into something quite a bit sleeker and more fitting for a princess of Liri.

But it was not to be.

For Dionysus had died before they could ever be married. Which had shifted her from the category of *future Princess*, to *unwanted ward*.

Dionysus's death had also hastened the demise of their father, his health failing him shortly after his youngest son died so tragically.

Which had moved Alexius from Prince to King.

Alex's duties as King had been immediate and pressing. The matter of Tinley not so. Her father was dead, and as she was the daughter of his father's most trusted advisor, her welfare had mattered a great deal. But it was nothing that he had to see to in the day today. However, now he was butting up against the reality of the will her father had left behind.

Alexius loved his father. And he had been very fond of Tinley's father as well. But it could not be said that either man was deeply entrenched in the modern era. No. In fact, it might be said—affectionately—that both men were a bit medieval. Again, not a problem for Alex. Until recently. But now that Tinley was approaching her twenty-third birthday, and about to go over the prescribed deadline for marriage, it was a problem. For he was tasked with finding a husband for Tinley.

The consequences of failing were unacceptable.

And he had vowed that he would take care of her. He had sworn it. His father had been on his deathbed when Dionysus had passed. And though he had not made accusations, the ferocity in his father's leonine gaze had sharpened as he looked at him.

For King Darius had been blessed with three sons. And only one had survived to the end of his life. Only one stood a chance at inheriting the throne. For Dionysus was dead, and Lazarus long before him. And the weight of the deaths of both rested on Alexius's shoulders.

The firstborn son in Liri was named successor to

the throne at birth, as it was with most other monarchies. But owed to years of war and corrupt leadership, there was a tradition.

All heirs of the King could issue challenges for the throne.

So while Alex had been born King, either of his brothers could challenge him at any time. Either to a battle, with the victor—either the last left alive, or the last to surrender—taking the throne.

Or there was the Dark Wood.

A week spent there, the last to surrender, or the one to emerge alive, named King.

The Lion of the Dark Wood.

And it was rumored that Alexius, even as a boy, had sought to end potential challengers to his throne.

King Darius had never accused him of such. His mother, on the other hand…

Things had changed.

And for all his life after, Alex had felt the distance between him and his mother. And the tension it had put between his mother and father.

What if he had been watching Lazarus more closely? What if he had stopped Dionysus that night he'd gone off drunk into the forest, rather than heeding his own selfish desires?

What if.

Some of his people revered Alexius as a god. He had, after all, met the challenge. Others saw him as fallible. A man who'd let those who should have been in his charge come to a tragic end. A man who had, perhaps, been born a ruthless, power-hungry monster.

Alexius had never known what his father believed. But the King had said to him, with a ferocity in his voice, that Tinley was now his responsibility. For her father was dead and her mother had never truly had the best interests of her daughter at heart.

I had thought for her to marry Dionysus. To honor her father's position in the country. But she was suited to be the wife of the spare, not the heir. She is fragile, that girl. Sweet. She needed your brother. Her father's wishes were that she marry, and the estate and money is tied up in his wishes. Find her a husband. Ensure she never wants for anything.

Alex had spoken nothing of Dionysus's flaws, for what would the point be? The King had had a blind spot when it came to his youngest son. He saw only the son, and none of the ways his selfish actions might have harmed Tinley.

But he'd asked Alex to ensure she wanted for nothing, and she hadn't.

Not a thing. In fact, he had made sure that she was able to attend a very prestigious University, where she had gotten a degree in social work. She currently held a position working for a charity, and he knew that while money meant very little to her on a personal level, she appreciated what she might accomplish with it in the broader world.

There was a clock ticking down. Tinley had to be married in her twenty-third year. If she was not, her father's money would be given to her next male relative.

It was funny to him, that his father thought Tinley suited Dionysus. Alex hadn't thought so. Tinley, though, had idolized Alex's brother. Had loved him. In the way a puppy loved its master, he'd often thought.

She'd had no idea he was dallying with other women, and happily, while Tinley was trailing after him, a flurry of ginger hair and pure devotion.

Watching it had made Alex's stomach sour.

"Yes," he said, his voice firm. "I was happy to allow you to live your life, but you have not come any closer to securing a marriage in the last four years than you were as a girl of eighteen."

"I was engaged at eighteen," she said softly.

"Younger," he said.

He looked around the cottage, which was something like a mishap out in the middle of the forest that had collected itself into four walls and a roof. There were baskets stacked in every corner, filled with yarn and what looked to be unspun wool.

The kitchen itself, which occupied the same space as the living area, was in a tip. There was a pie sitting on the counter, and there were baskets of blueberries, and flour sprinkled everywhere.

The woman herself had a bit of flour on her face.

As if the picture of spinster had not been painted well enough, a very large, fat ginger cat chose that moment to saunter into the room.

"To my point," he said. "You are no closer to finding a husband than you were four years ago. And I fear that you must. I wanted to keep my intervention to a minimum. But that is no longer practical."

She narrowed her eyes. "To *what* point?"

He let his gaze travel to the cat. "Nothing."

She frowned deeply and stood from the chair, making her way over to the beast. "Algernon is a rescue."

"I would've expected nothing less."

The cat walked by her, making a beeline straight for Alexius. The beast wove itself through his legs leaving behind a smattering of orange hair on his black pants.

"Retrieve your creature."

She huffed and crossed the space inelegantly, her softness amplified by her movements, her red hair a wild curl as she bent in a huff to pick up the massive mammal. "Leave the mean man alone, Algie. He hates cats. And sunshine. And rainbows. And everything good and proper in the world."

The problem with Tinley, the problem that had existed with Tinley since she'd begun to blossom into a woman, was that she was improbably beautiful. To him, at least. Her figure lush and soft, her hair untamed. She was unpredictable and unquenchable. She had freckles on her face and a gleam in her eyes that always seemed to hold a secret bit of humor. Her lips were full and quick with a smile, a wide smile that creased her cheeks and eyes and would make lines there when she was older.

She didn't seem concerned by it.

She rarely seemed concerned by anything.

And there was a part of him that had been drawn to that for years.

It was untenable. She was nothing like what he needed or wanted.

His body, though, had other thoughts about her, ridiculous though she was. A perversity in his nature.

"Need I remind you, Tinley. I am King. I am *your* King."

Tinley whirled in a circle, still holding her cat. "And I was going to be a princess."

"Not anymore."

Her mouth snapped shut, and her skin went waxen. "No."

"I'm not trying to be cruel, Tinley."

"Of course not. You don't have to try."

The moment stretched between them and he allowed it. She could despise him all she wanted. It wouldn't change the circumstances.

"So that's it. I marry, I get my inheritance. I don't marry. I don't get my inheritance. And not only do I not get the inheritance, my horrible cousin will get it, and he will likely spend the money on liquor and whores."

"That about sums it up."

"Well, that's just excellent. Anything more?"

"Yes. You leave Liri, and the palace withdraws its support."

The color drained from her face. "You would do that to me?"

"It's not I who wrote this will out, but your father, and mine."

"So what? They're dead, and you're the King. Surely you can override all of this."

He could not believe this *child* was arguing with him. He couldn't recall a time when anyone had dared. "I cannot. Because it was signed by the previous King. And these things are not that simple. And when it comes to you and your well-being, it is a matter of honor."

"Certainly not a matter of affection."

"Affection between you and I is inconsequential to me. But what is not is honoring that which my father has demanded of me. You must be cared for. And this is the way your father demanded you be cared for. I owe my father."

"Why, because you lost his other sons?"

She threw the challenge down with a resounding echo. She was the first one who had dared to lob such an accusation at him in a very long time. It was notable for that reason alone. And if he'd had a weak spot in that wrought iron chest of his it might have hurt.

But he was beyond hurt now.

Beyond feeling.

He was a man with drive, purpose. A man determined to become that which Liri required he be. He was prepared to do what needed to be done to honor his country and his father.

He too had a marriage time line. Though he was able to wait until thirty-five.

He had a prospective bride selected. A beautiful,

frosty socialite who had been trained for just such a position.

The very opposite of the explosion that was Tinley Markham. Tinley had been given every advantage that a socialite would have been, but she had always been... Well, she had always been unruly. The only child of Barabbas and Caroline Markham, she had been practically raised on the grounds of the palace. But her positioning as the future wife of his brother had certainly been more about his father's feelings regarding her father, than it had been about her particular suitability. The engagement had been cemented before Tinley had hit puberty.

And Tinley had... Well, she had worshipped Dionysus openly. And he had thought nothing of her. And why would he? She was a girl, and his brother Dionysus, four years her senior, was a renowned playboy with a voracious appetite for lush women. Blonde and ceramic or raven haired and brown skinned, he didn't much care. But he'd favored a particular sort. And in mass quantity. He had also favored drink.

It had been viewed as a lark. By his father, by the country. He was lighthearted. A man who knew how to enjoy a party.

Alexius had seen the darker side of Dionysus, even if no one else had.

It would be easy for Alex to name alcohol as the primary culprit in the death of his brother. Dionysus's obsession with sex and alcohol.

But then, Alex himself had known of those weaknesses in his brother. Had known what weaknesses they were.

And when, at a party where Tinley was in attendance, foxed out of his mind with a doe-eyed beauty clinging to his arm, Dionysus had claimed that he was going into the woods to face the spirits that had taken their brother, Alex should have known it would end badly.

He *had* known. On some level. For Lazarus had been lost in those same woods two years before Dionysus's birth and Alex should have had it in the forefront of his mind.

Instead…

Instead, that night, he'd made a different choice. He'd fallen prey to his own weaknesses. He'd sought to appease his own selfish desires. For the first time in his life, he'd truly thought only of himself. Consciously. Willingly.

And it had ended in tragedy.

His father had often said that his remaining sons were two sides of one coin. Their core was the same. Royal and resilient. They had the same golden eyes as their father that had earned him the name Lion of the Dark Wood. One that had become a title, along with King.

But Alex had always been missing the humor. The levity. And Dionysus had loved nothing more. He was named for the god of drink and revelry, after all.

It was their beautiful Greek mother who had named them, and she had done a fair job.

Except Lazarus was dead and wasn't returning.

And Dionysus's love of excess had in fact been his demise.

Alexius was simply…

He was simply King. And the rest was rumor, speculation, and in the case of Tinley, an inconvenience.

She held the cat clutched to her chest, and the creature left a gingery trail on her sweatshirt.

"I do hope you washed your hands before you made the pie."

"It's a cat friendly house."

The cat really was enormous. It spilled from Tinley's arms. "I suggest you find lodging for the beast. For you are returning to the palace with me."

He would not be ferrying himself back and forth between the palace and this badger's den she called a home. She was his project and he would have her in a convenient space.

Her eyes went round. "I will do no such thing."

"Leave your animals?"

"Return with you!"

"You haven't a choice, Tinley. I will see the stipulations of my father's last wishes fulfilled, and quickly."

She frowned. "And if I don't?"

"I will think nothing of using force, Tinley."

She frowned yet more deeply. "I am certain you would. All right. I will come. But my animals—"

"You cannot possibly think that you're bringing that into the royal palace of Liri."

"I fully think it. Your father had dogs."

"He did. Dogs that would have...eaten *that*."

"Algie is coming with me."

"Algie," he repeated, the word dripping with disdain.

"They're *all* coming with me."

He narrowed his gaze. *"All?"*

"Yes. Peregrine, Alton and Nancy."

"Are they all cats?"

"Don't be ridiculous."

He regarded her expression, which had gone mulish. "I'm sorry. I don't know how to respond to that."

"Peregrine is a ferret. Alton and Nancy are hedgehogs."

"I live in a palace, not a menagerie."

"I thought my happiness was important to you. I have a life. I have a charity to run. I have rescue animals."

"I suggest you open the cages and release the animals into your garden. Hedgehogs are often quite happy in gardens. I have it on good authority they can often be heard rutting beneath windows, so it must be a happy place for them."

Tinley's face went beetroot. "You of all people should know that it's dangerous out in the woods." Her eyes clashed with his, sparks in their green depths.

And he was done sparring with an impotent creature.

"I will bring my men in to pack up your detritus." He looked around at all of the baskets. "Do you require...everything?"

"Yes," she said. "I do require everything. If I don't have my yarn I won't be able to knit."

"God forbid. We cannot have a knitting crisis."

"Indeed. You say that dryly, but you have no idea. Also, we should bring the pie."

She looked around. "I'm able to work on my charity remotely."

"It will please you to learn the castle has Wi-Fi."

"Really? I'm somewhat surprised."

"Why are you surprised?"

"Because nothing about you seems modern, Alex."

Though on the outside, he remained stone, her words hit him strangely. He could not recall the last time a person had called him *Alex*.

His brother had done. Everyone else referred to him as Your Majesty. No one was so bold as to be quite so familiar with him. But of course, Tinley would be.

She would have heard her father refer to him as such. Alex walked to the window of the cottage and waved his hand. It was a signal for his men to come, and come they did. They descended on the small cottage and made quick work of everything in it. But by the time they had done so, he and Tinley, and a carrier that contained Algie, were bundled up in the back of the sleek black town car.

"He does not like to travel," she said. "If he couldn't hear my voice he would be very cross."

"Tinley, do not mistake me, I am doing this for my own convenience. You have to marry."

"Have to. So much have to in your world and I would have thought I'd escaped it when your brother died, but no. Here we are. Trying to get me to conform with all this protocol."

A wealth of memory flashed between them. Every time he'd ever scolded her for breaking that protocol.

He could remember clearly the time she had come with his family on a vacation to the Amalfi Coast. And she'd worn some swimming costume that was horrendously inappropriate. One piece but plunging down to her breast bone, the cut around her legs coming up over her hips.

He'd been entranced by her body.

And it had angered him.

The press makes it their mission to get photographs of our family outings. You must be conscious of that, Tinley.

What's wrong with this? It's not a bikini, and this isn't the Dark Ages! Should I make sure I'm covered from crown to ankle?

You are to be my brother's wife. You must conduct yourself with a bit of decorum.

Then perhaps you ought to cover yourself. What will the world do if it gets a glimpse of your royal chest hair?

She'd planted her palm in the center of his chest to give him a shove and he'd caught her wrist, their eyes locking together.

And he'd nearly been lost then. He'd been able to see clearly that Tinley had no idea why their eyes made sparks when they clashed. Why the air suddenly felt thick.

But he knew.

He knew and she didn't. And it was all the reason he'd needed to release her.

Protocol had not come into it.

"Well. It's a shame that your protocol wasn't functioning when you let Dionysus get lost in the woods."

"I did not over consume alcohol on my brother's behalf. Neither did I beseech him to try and impress the equally drunk and luxuriously curvy woman he was with." He knew that was unkind. To bring up the woman. That betrayal had hurt Tinley then. He didn't care. He couldn't afford to care. And he had no patience with her accusations. "And finally, I did not direct a pack of wolves to tear him limb from limb."

He felt something in his chest that might have been pain once. But the years had left him too hard and scarred to feel it.

He wore grief like a cloak. As much a part of him as the crown. It was not painful. It was not sad. It simply was. There was a weight to it, but it was not unbearable.

The grief for Dionysus, though, it was tinged with anger.

For he should have known better.

He knew the stories of how Lazarus had vanished.

He had gone in anyway. Brash and bold to impress a woman. For the forest would surely deem him worthy. As everyone had deemed that golden child, born after the King and Queen's first loss.

Worthy, more than worthy. Invincible.

But it had proven not to be so.

Dionysus had been lost in the wood, cementing Alex's reign as inevitable. Cementing his reputation as a fated ruler.

It was the Lion who remained. The Lion who claimed the throne.

The Lion who now found himself alone with the woman who had once been his brother's. Soft and delicate. And not for him.

It was all a bit gothic.

"How can you talk about it like that? You don't have a heart."

"No," he said, and that at least was true. It had been replaced with granite long ago. And without a heart, all he could fathom was duty.

Tinley was a duty. No matter how she might try him.

Her animals, her yarn, everything she came with. They would be his problem for just a little while longer.

"But I do have the means to find you a husband. And I will do so, Tinley, you have my word. I will return to you that which I stole from you. I will find you a husband. You have my word."

CHAPTER TWO

TINLEY HADN'T BEEN back to the palace since King Darius's funeral. It had been just two weeks after Dionysus's funeral and she'd been shocked the palace hadn't crumbled around them all.

To lose both of them so quickly had been... It had been unthinkable, and yet it had been real.

Her life had felt like an absolute parade of grief. One blow after another. Her father. Her fiancé. The man she'd thought of as an uncle.

Her mother was still alive. She had her mother, but...they had never been...close. She had always been such a disappointment to her mother.

When King Darius had told her that she would marry Prince Dionysus she'd been so honored. She'd been young enough she hadn't fully understood what married meant. But she'd felt...approved of. She'd felt special.

Her mother had been so upset. Why Dionysus? Why not Alexius? Why not the future King?

A princess, not a queen. A slight, her mother had said.

Because of her tromping footsteps, frizzy hair and dizzy demeanor.

That was the first time she'd realized her mother had had loftier plans for her than she would ever reach. The first time she'd realized she would never be what her mother wanted.

Their distance had not improved in the years since.

Tinley had felt like she might as well not have a family, while her mother had gone to Italy and joined a fashionable crowd there.

Her engagement then might not have been all her mother had wanted, but it had brought Tinley into the fold of the royal family and from the time she was eight onward she lived in the palace part-time, along with her father who acted as advisor to the King. When he was there, she was too. They went on family vacations, attended royal balls and ate dinner with the family.

She'd been besotted with Dionysus from the moment she'd learned he was to be her husband.

He was beautiful, and kind. Closer to her age than Alexius, who frightened her. And who never smiled. Who always seemed to disapprove of her and who had not gotten less forbidding, but more so once she became a teenager.

Still, she'd been happy with her engagement.

But second best would never be good enough for her mother.

Her parents had been older when her mother had finally fallen pregnant with her. She'd been like a fairy tale gift and her mother had built up a store of expectations for what that might mean.

But she had been her father's pride and joy. Just as she was.

Then she'd lost him. And the other two men in her life who'd meant the very most to her.

Illness had taken her father, and the King.

Dionysus had been taken so cruelly she…she couldn't even allow herself to think of that night. It was too painful.

So she had left Liri. She had immersed herself in her new life. In University. In the friendships she'd made there. The new hobbies she had discovered.

She had joined clubs. She had learned to bake. She had taken knitting lessons from an older woman who lived near the University. She had enjoyed her years in Boston. She had experienced new food, new culture, and she had escaped.

But it had never been real. Because marriage was the end destination for her, whether she wanted it to be or not.

Or else she'd be exiled in poverty, which wasn't a great option.

She had returned to Liri six months ago somewhat reluctantly, but there was a cottage there waiting for her, and she had known that. She had also been given the opportunity to head up a charitable foundation that contributed to the education of special needs children. The combination had been irresistible. So home she had gone.

Home.

After the death of King Darius, that final loss of the familiar life… Liri hadn't felt like home.

But the cottage had begun to feel like home.

This palace…

She had spent weeks at a time there sometimes.

It was a second home, and she had moved between her parents' grand manor home in the Lirian city of Tanaro and this castle with ease.

She'd felt happier here than there. For a time.

Coming back she felt nothing like happy at all.

It had been strange to come back to Liri at all, moving into the cottage near the edge of the wood.

There was dark magic at the center of the wood, and she knew it. Every Lirian child knew it.

And the palace overlooked the Dark Wood. This forest that had taken the love of her life away.

Even now, it made her heart ache.

She had been promised to Prince Dionysus since she was eight years old, and he was twelve. She had fallen in love with him when she'd turned fourteen.

A smile from him had been worth a pound of gold. More. She had thought he was the most beautiful, brilliant man. She had tried to explain her situation to some friends when she'd been at school, and they had all been horrified, that two children had been promised in marriage to each other. But they didn't know the truth of it. They didn't know him. They didn't understand how handsome he was. They were imagining some kind of medieval arrangement, but it hadn't been. The affection between their fathers had been real.

The honor it had been, for her anyway…it had been real.

And the way that she had felt for him had been… Well, it had been equally real.

The idea of getting married now…

She didn't want to. Her life was a monument to the loss of Dionysus. She was trying to be useful in the position she found herself in. In many ways it was better that she not be a princess, she supposed.

She knew he hadn't been… She knew there had been other women.

And yes, she'd been disappointed there had still been other women, even when she was old enough that he might have turned his attentions to her.

But he was gone. And there was no real reason to hate him for being with another woman when he died. He'd never been with her anyway. He'd never made any promises.

She chose to remember the things she'd loved about him.

She wouldn't have been suited to being a princess, though. And she wasn't really suited to marriage at all, she didn't think. Her path had been determined for her from a young age, and because of that there were some things she'd never really thought about it.

Really, she had never thought of what it meant to be a princess. Only what it would be like to walk down the vast Cathedral aisle in a white dress toward the man her heart had longed for ever since she had understood why men and women were different.

The reality of it… Well, it fairly horrified her.

She had discovered that she liked to work behind the scenes. Doing hair and makeup just frustrated her. It reminded her of how frustrated she made her mother. Whenever she and her father had been back in residence in the family home, or when her mother had come for stints at the palace, her mother had picked at her.

Reminded her of all of her shortcomings.

She'd told her King Darius and her father might have been accepting of her in the role of Princess, but the press would have been vicious. She would have been subjected to millions of people scrutinizing her as her mother did and the idea of that was... intolerable.

Apart from the reasons she didn't like the idea of being looked at, she had also discovered that she liked quiet evenings at home. That she was good at particular things, just not socialite and royalty things. She had an artistic flair that she didn't discover until she went to University, and she expressed that through her baking, and with her knitting.

Losing Dionysus had been a tragedy. But from that, she had discovered some deep and important parts of herself. And somehow coming back here... It made it feel like that new creation she'd knit herself into was all beginning to unravel.

She was wearing leggings and a sweatshirt.

She hadn't been expecting Alexius to come to her house today. But Alexius didn't announce himself. He didn't ask permission, and he didn't make plans. He simply was.

It had been like that when she'd been at University. He'd come to see her three times, with no warning each time.

And good luck explaining why a man who radiated regal bearing and who was so handsome he made women swoon in the dorm halls, had come to see her.

Well, she'd had to just explain.

She was the ward of the King of her home country. As simple and complicated as that.

Just like the current situation.

She had seen the paperwork, and there was no use arguing.

She needed the money. Not for herself, but to fund the charity. Well, she did need to live, as well. Have money to feed her animals…

But the idea of a husband…

She was well used to the idea of an arranged marriage. It was just that the first one that had been arranged had suited her so much.

"I have a few requests."

Alex turned and looked at her, and there was something about that stark, rock carved expression that made her stomach feel hollow.

He was such a large man. Having him in her cottage had been strange and disorienting. He was so firmly associated with a life that she had left behind. With the forbidding palace walls.

That was why he made her feel so strange.

He always had. So grim and dark and brooding. A long shadow cast over her sunny days at the castle.

He had never thought she was good enough for his brother. Her mother was angry with her for failing to be good enough to be Queen.

Alexius had never even thought her good enough to be Princess.

She doubted he thought she was good enough to scrub the floors.

"Requests?"

He was looking at her as if she'd grown a second head. One he didn't like any more than the first.

"If you're going to help me find a husband..."

"It isn't going to just be any husband. He must meet the requirements that I know your father would have."

She could say no. But he would only force her to go with him. There was no point opposing him here and now. Maybe she would be able to regroup at the palace, or perhaps they could come to an understanding after she met with some of his suggestions. But arguing now would get her nowhere.

She was too familiar with the brick wall that was Alexius to bother trying.

"Fine. But find me...the most bookish aristocrat you can. A man with a library. A man who likes to stay home in the evenings. A man who likes cats."

"I'm afraid our criteria are different, Tinley."

"*My* criteria have to matter," she said.

"I could easily find you a noble who doesn't care what you do."

"True."

The idea of that kind of marriage filled her with

a great unease. Her parents had been a bit like that. Tinley was absolutely wild about her father. Her mother had always been untouchable. A beautiful doll in a glass case. There had been a distance between the two of them that could be felt when you were standing with them.

She had never wanted that. And she had been convinced that she and Dionysus wouldn't. Because he had looked at her and her insides had lit up.

Given the way he'd died… She knew that there were other women. She hadn't thought about it, not until then. Not until that poor traumatized girl in the woods, who had watched him die while she'd hidden.

But before then she simply hadn't thought about that. She'd considered the chasteness in their relationship a sign of his respect for her. Their engagement had felt like something enchanted, just like the forest.

But the forest had swallowed him whole.

The magic had not been with them after all.

She had been so sure that things between them would be different. And then she had been ready to spend the rest of her life… Well, not alone. She had friends. She had a calling, more than a job. She had found a niche. She had found some happiness.

Alexius had come in and upended it.

It's your father's will…

She couldn't even take that on board.

Alex was also sadly right. Of course there were any number of aristocratic men who would be happy to have a distant relationship with their wife. Who would expect to continue having affairs in the way that they saw fit. Who would maintain cordial politeness, and allow her to use their money and her money.

"I fail to see how that's me being taken care of. And I feel certain that if my father were alive…"

"I cannot negotiate with a dead man, Tinley. This document is written as law."

The car stopped, but it wasn't the driver who ended up opening the door for Tinley, but Alexius himself. She moved slowly out of the vehicle, staring up at him. He was more than a head taller than his brother had been, and much, much broader. Dionysus had been a manageable fantasy with an easy smile.

Alexius was not a fantasy. He was a mountain.

One she had no desire to be standing at the base of.

She moved quickly, clutching Algernon's carrier to her chest.

"Wait," he said, his voice weighted with authority. And she had no choice but to stop.

There was something about that voice. It traveled down her spine like lightning and immobilized her.

"I will accompany you."

He held his arm out to her, and she, out of force of a long forgotten habit, looped her arm around his, and allowed him to lead her toward the front doors of the palace. She felt ridiculous. She was wearing trainers, leggings and a sweatshirt, next to a man in a bespoke suit. She was holding a cat carrier.

And this had once been her life. This place. There

was a time when she had been the presumptive Princess and…

She could hardly reconcile it with who she was now.

The palace loomed before them as they walked up the brick path, and the wind picked up, wrapping her in a breeze that seemed to be full of memory, grief and a strange longing that seemed to well up from deep inside of her.

She wanted to hide. She wanted to jump in the cat carrier with Algernon.

But she didn't. She kept her gaze steady, and she kept walking. Like she didn't look a ridiculous mess. Like she wasn't a frizzy-haired woman walking with a polished king.

She felt like she was living in an alternate moment. And when the grand doors opened wide, and they entered the great antechamber that she knew led to the throne room, her heart squeezed so tight she thought she would choke.

"Welcome back," he said.

She looked around the space, and she felt decidedly…

It was a strange feeling. It wasn't bad or good.

"Charis," he said, as a woman entered the room. "Please show Tinley to her room."

The momentary relief that she felt over being out of Alex's presence was completely replaced by the disquiet that she felt moving through the once familiar hallways.

She could see her father everywhere. She could see King Darius.

She looked up at the walls, and she saw portraits of the family. Hanging on those marble walls.

She had never known Lazarus. He had died long before she was born.

But oh, she remembered the rest of them.

The Queen had been beautiful, but frail. And everyone said that she wasn't the same after Lazarus disappeared.

They had also said that it was a blessing she had died before her youngest son.

Before her husband.

Because the grief would have just been a cruelty she could never have borne.

As she moved down the hallway, looking at all the portraits, her gaze kept landing on those of Alexius. He was intense. Dark and brooding, even in these depictions. He was so different than Dionysus. And she had never really felt like…

Not that either of them had ever been her playmates, or anything of the sort. She had been an inconvenience, underfoot to them. Dionysus had been kind to her, likely because he knew that she would be his wife someday. Kind, a bit indulgent.

Alexius had always been…remote. Distant.

In fact, he reminded her of the wood.

And it seemed fitting, because it was the wood that had consumed the man that she was meant to marry.

And it was the man who seemed like a personification of that dark, demonic place that had brought her here.

The room had a familiar feel to it, but she couldn't quite be certain that she had ever stayed in it before. But it had a massive canopy bed. And it overlooked the lake, not the forest. For which she was grateful.

"Charis," she said to the woman, as she retreated. "Can you please make sure that my… That my other animals are brought to me." She paused for a moment. "And my yarn."

"Of course," she said.

When the woman retreated, Tinley put the cat carrier down on the bed and opened the door.

Algie did not come out. In fact, he seemed peevish over the change in scenery. "This is a palace," she said, keeping her voice soft. "You're supposed to like it better than the cottage."

He meowed plaintively.

"I know," she said softly. "I don't either."

When her things were brought to her, she was all ready to settle in for the evening. But before Charis left her with Nancy, Alton and Peregrine, she paused at the door. "I'll be back in a moment with your dress. We are going to have to get you ready for dinner."

CHAPTER THREE

SHE WAS LATE. And Alexius did not like to be kept waiting. At least, he didn't *think* he liked to be kept waiting.

No one had ever dared do it before.

If he were not so angry, he might find it extraordinary.

Of course for Tinley it was par for the course.

She always dared.

His mind flashed back to her pushing him. Her hand on his chest...

The door to the dining room opened, and the creature that appeared there was nearly unrecognizable. That cloud of carrot hair had been tamed into something sleek. He could not see her freckles, smoothed by some sort of makeup. Her lips were painted a pink color that should have clashed with her hair, but somehow didn't.

Her gown was much the same. A daring shade that went off the shoulder and revealed far more creamy skin than he was comfortable seeing on her.

He hated it.

It was not Tinley. And yet it was. Her voluptuous figure on display, her full lips dewy from some gloss that verged on pornographic.

She was a nightmare. Tinley made visually acceptable as if to mock the fact he found her attractive even when she didn't. And to present to him a vision of her as the sort of sleek trophy he was seeking in a queen.

She couldn't know, and yet there was a light in her green eyes that spoke to him. That said: Where are your excuses now?

Not a girl.

Not dizzy.

Not frizzy.

"Good evening," she said, edging slowly into the room and taking a seat a comical ten chairs away from him.

His body relaxed into the relief of the distance and he tightened his fist. Unwilling to cede that he needed her to keep distance.

"Tinley," he said. "We will not be able to discuss anything if you are half a league away from me."

"Sorry," she said. "I didn't know the appropriate distance to keep from a king."

He thought of the times they had all been forced to dine at one end of the table, with their fathers down at the other talking about matters of state.

She knew well enough.

"When you are dining with a king you must sit close enough to converse with him," he said.

"Well, your voice *does* carry."

"It shouldn't have to."

She stood, hardly the picture of lithe grace and dignity. No. She was nothing half so basic.

You want basic. You need it.

She walked slowly over to where he was. And then she sat, her posture remaining comically rigid.

"I'm surprised you didn't bring the cat."

She rolled her eyes at him. Like a bratty teen. "I'm not ridiculous."

"Good to know."

Those same eyes now narrowed at him. "Was that a joke?"

"No. It really is helpful to know that you're not ridiculous. It's valuable to know exactly what it is I'm working with."

"It may have escaped your notice," she said, folding her hands in front of her on the table and staring him down. "But I am not eighteen. I'm not eight years old, either. I run and coordinate a charity. I manage events, fund-raisers. I'm not going to bring a cat to the dinner table."

And in those words he saw a spark of something. Not just the dizzy, frizzy hair that he had noticed earlier. But the light deep down inside of her that he was certain she must show in other areas of her life. She had to. If not, then how could she run a charity.

When he had arrived at the cottage and seen it in disarray, when he had taken a look around at all the homey things that—in his opinion—were a study in superfluity, he knew that many people saw the life of a Royal as one of potential excess. Of privilege.

And it was true, there was a great deal of power and privilege to be had when one was royal.

But in Liri, at least, the tradition of royalty ran much more toward stark. The King was the protector. Liri had mountains to the north, the sea to the south, and thick forest to the east and west, guarding the borders, with Italy on one side and Slovenia on the other. They were small, but they were powerful. And the ruler of the country had always been a part of that power.

It was not power to be taken lightly.

His father had taught him that a king must rule with a firm hand.

He and Dionysus were different people. He had always been more serious than his brother. And it was entirely possible that… Perhaps his brother would have brought some much-needed lightness to the country.

His father had been an only child, and Alex knew it had been his hope that his sons would help one another. That they would not have the competition seen in family generations past, but that Dionysus would be the piece Alexius might be missing on his own.

The world was not as it had once been, after all.

The Lion of the Dark Wood had been necessary across the history of Liri. They'd had conflict with other nations. They had struggled financially in the beginning. War, famine.

These things were not so in the twilight of his father's reign, and they were not so for Alexius.

But he was what the people had gotten. Even if he was not what they deserved.

And he was what Tinley had to contend with as well. Whether she liked it or not.

"It is true," he said, "that you have managed to tame yourself into an image that will be easier for me to pass off to another gentleman."

"That's very sweet that you think of yourself as a gentleman."

"A figure of speech, more than an actual commentary on my beliefs regarding myself."

Her eyes glittered.

She was a strange and fascinating creature. She seemed hapless, and yet he could see that wasn't the case. Her choices, her animals, her hair…

There was a deliberateness to her. To the hodge-podge of her house and the whirlwind of her movements. And he realized she wasn't dizzy at all.

She was like a carnival ride, flashing and spinning and lighting up the night. Seemingly random and reckless, but in fact spinning in perfectly calculated time.

It was like he was seeing her for the first time. Not as he wanted to call her. It was easier to just see her as accidental, for that made her less than she was.

And she was already far too much.

But she was right. She could not do the job she did, couldn't have graduated from University, if she were truly haphazard.

"Tell me," he said, the command in his voice like

iron. For his every command was iron. "What was it like to grow up with your father?"

She blinked. "Why?"

"Because I'm intrigued. I'm interested in what exactly has made you…this. You were raised practically in the palace, as I was."

"As was Dionysus," she said. "But the two of you could not be more different than… Well, a Ferrari and a lion."

"Those comparisons have nothing in common."

"To my point," she said, dryly mimicking something he'd said to her earlier. "You know, one is machinery. Modern and sleek and shiny. The other is a bit toothy. Dangerous. Ancient."

"If that's a joke about my age…"

"Oh, no." She waved a hand. "It's definitely about your personality."

"So tell me. How is it you managed to grow into… what you are?"

"You saw me grow up. I was here most of the time."

"And when you weren't?"

She blinked. "I don't know. I guess… It was difficult with my mother. Always. I think she loves me."

She looked away, her eyes downcast.

"You *think*?"

She looked back at him, her expression defiant. "Yes. I think she withheld her praise because she thought if she gave it I might not try. And in her opinion I never tried hard enough."

He felt…he didn't like it, for he *felt*. But he knew what it was to be denied your mother's love. He knew.

"Tried hard enough for what?" he asked.

"To be… Well, to be her, I suppose."

Her mother had always seemed spoiled and selfish to him. Certainly nothing like Tinley. And nothing she could ever want to be.

"If I remember correctly. You really are nothing like your mother."

She shook her head. "No. And I also think she was very disappointed that I wasn't… Well, that I wasn't asked to be your wife."

"My wife?"

"Princess is a bit below Queen, particularly in the estimation of my mother, who I think believed that our fathers' connections would benefit us more than she believed it did in the end."

"So my brother wasn't good enough for her?"

"Mostly, I'm not good enough for her. But the thing is, I was more than good enough for my father. I loved him so much. And he loved me." She looked down at her plate. "Your father picked me for Dionysus just like I was. It was much easier to be more of that person than the woman who could never be the Queen my mother wanted me to be."

He knew what it was to disappoint a mother. More than disappoint. He might as well have taken a knife and cut his mother open.

He should have been the one to be keeping an eye on his brother.

They had been outside playing on the palace

grounds, and it wasn't until he realized he no longer heard his brother laughing that he realized something was wrong. He had lifted his head to see the back of his brother as he disappeared into the Dark Wood. As the trees seemed to swallow him whole. He had run after him. With all of his speed and might, but he was nowhere to be found.

Not a trace of Lazarus had ever been found.

He had only been seven years old, but Alexius had searched for his brother in the wood with the men until he had nearly fallen off the mount with exhaustion.

And then, he had gone back out the next day, after forty-five minutes of sleep, to continue searching. He had gone into the wood, and no harm had become of him.

The Lion of the Dark Wood. Or, a failure who had allowed his brother to die.

Opinion was divided.

Not with his mother, though.

He was thankful yet again that she had not lived through the death of Dionysus, for her opinion would've been confirmed then.

"And you...you were born a mountain?" She asked.

"I was born to be King. But time changes us all."

She shook her head. "You've always been like this."

"Regretfully, I cannot speak to the way that you've always been." But he could. For he could remember her, a ball of energy and light and noise.

And could remember her as she grew older, watching the energy shift and change into something that shone from her eyes, rather than exploding into uncontrolled movement.

That was when the feeling in him had begun to shift. From a fascination that verged on horror that his father had chosen her as wife of the spare, to an attraction that felt like an abomination.

It felt no less so now.

"Why should you?" she asked. "I was nothing more than a child to you. But of course when you're seventeen or so you don't think you're a child, do you?"

He locked his jaw tight. "I wasn't."

That truth stood stark between them. "I don't suppose you were."

"We do a great deal of supposing between the two of us."

"No need," she said. "We can confirm. That's my origin story. A girl who was told she would be a princess at eight. Whose mother found that to be a disappointment. Who was frizzy and loud, and still is." She reached up and touched her sleek locks. "Your staff did sort of an amazing job fixing me up. I can't take credit for it. I've never known what to do with my hair."

"Well, if you marry wealthy enough you shall never have to. You either hire the appropriate staff who will enable it to look however you wish, or you'll be able to keep it as is and call it a trend, as your hus-

band will be influential enough that you will command such public opinion."

"Not a dream that I've ever had. But I would like
very much to command influence to help with my
charity."

"Why does that charity matter to you?"

"I was very lucky. No matter who I might have
been born, or how, I would have been able to get
an education. My safety net has always been…well,
you. A king. When I left this country, when I began
talking to people about their different experiences,
people from all over the world who I met at school, I
realized that that wasn't true for most of them. That if
they were there, it was often through great financial
expense of their parents, or an immense amount of
effort. More than a normal person could ever give. If
a person has learning disabilities, or special needs,
the fight that they're engaged in to get the kind of
education that will work for them is intense. And it's
education that enables them to take their place in the
world. We want people to work. We want them to be
productive members of society, but we don't care to
give them the building blocks in order to make that
happen. I do care. For people who are not as fortu-
nate as I've been."

"I hope that's the speech that you give at events
for your charity."

"More or less."

"It's very affecting."

"Thank you. I've discovered that I care quite a bit

about it as a topic. Accidents of birth shouldn't be the deciding factor in your potential."

"Neither should accidents of death. But my life has certainly been changed by them." Normally, he would not have made such a comment, but he was struck by the strange realization that he and Tinley shared commonalities he would never have imagined.

Though, she had not earned her mother's disdain.

She looked at him, those green eyes full of a deep, round emotion he couldn't put a name to. A suspicious sort of question that stopped short of accusation, but held no small amount of censure.

She looked down, her neat white teeth closing over her lip. "Why didn't you stop him from going into the woods?"

She could have been speaking of either of his brothers. Either of his historic failures.

"Should I? That is a common take, Tinley, and you're not the first to express it. Though most don't express it directly to me. I should have stopped both of my brothers from going in the woods, shouldn't I? And yet, I did go in after them. And I seem to have emerged unscathed."

"So, you believe that you're the Lion of the Dark Wood? The born leader of this nation? Fated to rule and any potential competition removed?"

"I believe nothing of the kind. I believe that if you're drunk and a fool and you go running into the woods where your older brother previously disappeared, and where you know there are packs of hungry wolves, you are perhaps taking your chances."

"That's a disrespectful way to speak of the dead."

"The dead got themselves eaten by wolves. The dead must be strong enough to cope with the fact that unflattering things will be said about them."

She frowned deeply. "The dead is not here to defend himself."

"If he were, do you think he would defend himself? No. He would smile, and he would take another drink. For all that I find him frustrating, I cannot hate him. For he is entirely who he is. At least, he was."

"It's what I liked about him," she said softly. "There was a freedom to him that I admired. And I tried to carry it forward in my life. I did. I tried to be… I tried to be someone he would have liked."

"He was young. And I do not believe he knew quite what he liked, or what he would have liked had he been able to grow more. I think eventually, he would have liked you quite a lot." Those last few words were rough in his throat. Painful.

Their food arrived at that moment, wheeled in on carts by members of his staff. And as her plate was set out before her, he continued. "In any case, I've taken you on."

"Wonderful," she snapped. "So, I've gone from prospective Princess to charity case. Unless of course you want to make my mother's hopes and dreams come true and make me your Queen?"

She was being provocative on purpose. And she didn't think he'd rise to meet her.

"And if I did?"

His words were like a gauntlet thrown down between them and their eyes clashed for a moment and something…electric passed through the air.

Down his spine.

He resented it. The tightness in his chest, his gut. That she should have the power to change the air around him. That the air would change without his permission.

"No thank you," she said.

He was nearly disappointed that she backed down.

She looked down at her plate.

Then she looked back up at him, delight suddenly shining from those green eyes.

He felt that delight pour through him like melted gold. Hot and precious and dangerous. Something strange that went off low in his stomach. Like a bomb bursting.

The food. The food had made her light up like a switch had been turned on and there was something inescapably compelling about her simple joy.

No.

She was in love with his dead brother.

He was the King.

She would never be his Queen.

"Dinner looks amazing," she said. "Is that puff pastry?"

She poked at the top of the meat pie sitting on her plate. *Poked* at it.

He said nothing.

"It's lovely," she said, cutting through the top of it, and closing her eyes when the crust made a sound. "Amazing." She hummed as she took a bite.

There was something to the excitement in her. The warmth. This castle was ancient, a stack of stones that had come from a cold earth. And she infused them with…her. He could feel her. Surrounding him. How long had it been since he'd seen someone take pleasure in such a simple thing?

There was a purity in her that ran through his veins and twisted. Turned from that bright innocence of a woman enjoying the flavor of her dinner, into something dark and tortured in him.

She looked up at him. "What?"

"Absolutely nothing," he said.

He looked away. Perhaps it had been too long since he'd had a woman. He had been focused on the practicalities of striking a deal with Nadia. The two of them had no connection, physical or otherwise, and she had been out of the country for the entirety of the negotiations. Given that he was in the process of negotiating a marriage agreement, he had not thought it prudent to take a lover. But perhaps in this case a discreet lover would be the better part of valor.

He could not endure this. This proximity to her.

It was a sickness that should have died the night his brother did.

But here it endured.

"Next week. Next week we will have a ball, and we will invite all of the eligible men in the higher echelons of society, from all nations friendly to Liri. And there, we will find you a husband."

"That makes me a bit like Prince Charming, doesn't it?"

"If any of the men arrive in a pumpkin I'll be sure to let you know."

"You know, I would quite like that. Because not only would he come with a pumpkin, he would come with a couple of fat rats. And I assume his suit would be tailored by birds."

"That's absurd."

"It's been said, on more than one occasion, that I myself am slightly absurd. So, that bothers me less than you think it might."

"Your cat would eat them," he pointed out.

"We can't have that. Though, he has not eaten the hedgehogs or the ferret yet."

"A relief to all involved."

"You know," she said, and impish expression taking over her face. "If it happens now, I'm going to blame the change of venue."

"The death of your rodents will weigh heavily upon my conscience."

And he realized that perhaps it was a poor choice of words, considering there were two deaths that did weigh upon his conscience. Deaths that the passage of time would never ease the wounds of. Deaths that had caused deep and abiding division in his country. Between the people who supported him still, and the people who thought him a murderer.

Division that he was having to work now to ease.

"End of the week," he said. "There will be a ball. You will behave. You will comply."

"What if I didn't?"

The question was asked so simply, the expression on her face not angry or inflammatory in any way. Rather it simply was. A sort of innocent wonderment that he had only ever witnessed in Tinley.

"I would throw you in the dungeon."

"You could just marry me and save us the trouble."

"In the end," he said, his stomach going tight. "Dungeon or marriage to me. Is there a difference?"

She shook her head slowly. "No. There isn't."

After that, there was no more conversation.

And by the time she left the dinner table, a knot had begun to form in his chest that only expanded with each passing moment. And when she left the room, it did not ease.

The sooner he had Tinley Markham married off the better.

He got up from his seat and went over to the bar that was at the far end of the massive dining room. He took out a bottle of scotch and poured himself a measure of it. He downed it in one gulp.

The sooner she was dealt with, the sooner he could get on with the business of ruling Liri.

And the sooner he would have fat cats and hedge-hogs removed from his castle.

That would be a blessing indeed.

CHAPTER FOUR

COMPORTMENT LESSONS BEGAN the next day. Tinley was horrified. Why was he so hell-bent on changing her? Yes, there had been a presumption that if she was going to be Princess she would have to conform in some way. But she had assumed that her basic raw material was decent, considering she had been chosen to be the Princess of Liri at a very early age.

And anyway, that future was gone. She wasn't supposed to be a princess. She was simply looking for a...for a husband.

She looked around the ballroom, empty except for the older woman that Alex had assigned to be her mentor.

She had been walking with a book on her head for half an hour.

But for some reason, every time she got midway through the room she would imagine Alex's dark, disapproving gaze boring a hole through her, and she would stumble.

She really didn't like him.

Their conversation last night had been strange. It had affected her in unexpected ways.

It had been easy to cast him as the villain in Dionysus's death. Though the ferocity of her anger had waned over the years.

She had gotten older, and as she had borne witness to rowdy, drunken behavior in college, she had been forced to ask herself many times who needed to bear responsibility for that behavior.

And every time, she could only ever bestow the responsibility to the people engaging in the behavior.

Which meant Dionysus bore the weight of his own rash act.

He had been twenty-two years old when he'd died. He had seemed such a man to her. Now that she was the same age as he'd been when he passed it seemed…strange. Because they were on equal footing now.

And she… Well, she would not have done the things he did. She wouldn't have drunk to excess and put herself in danger like that.

She would never have cheated.

The thought of that was like a knife twisting her chest. Not because she loved him so much. Not now. It was just…she'd excused it. A great many times, because it hadn't suited the vision she'd had of him, of her feelings for him, to be angry about the other women.

But it had been wrong.

She couldn't imagine Alex behaving in such a way. Never.

Alex had been in his own stratosphere to her when Dionysus had died. In his thirties already and so remote and responsible. She'd been certain then it was all age, and now she knew better.

She didn't know why she was comparing the two of them. Dionysus had been fun. Dynamic. He'd had plans for the country in his role as Prince, and when he had spoken, it had been electric. He had been a firm favorite of the people for a variety of reasons. He had established festivals and parades. He had brought a much-needed levity to the culture.

She loved her country. She always had.

Her mother was American, and she had spent a great deal of time in the States as a girl, and had also been privileged enough to travel around the world. She felt that gave her the context to truly appreciate Liri and what was unique about it. But she could also appreciate the fact that it had an old-fashioned feel to it, that there was a sense of seriousness derived from years spent with the people in poverty, and with uncertainty surrounding them while war had raged.

There had been generations of that sort of unrest, all resolved when King Darius had been in power. But the psyche of the people was rooted in that, and those things did not change overnight.

Dionysus had seemed like the medicine the country needed.

It had seemed as if he had been born not feeling the weight of the potential crown. And it had been a good thing.

Alex himself seemed to bear the weight of a

mountain on his shoulders. And he walked straight and tall all the same. But there was…a gravity to him that seemed to affect the rotation of her when she was around him.

It was disconcerting at best. But then, this entire situation was disconcerting. Because she had spent a few years feeling like she might be a normal girl. Not one who had been set on the rarest and strangest of paths as a child, only to be completely derailed from it, then spat out into the real world alone and aimless.

But she'd had a chance to rebuild herself from the ground up. In Boston, there had been no expectations, no decisions about her future made anymore.

And in the back of her mind she'd known about the stipulations in her father's will but it had seemed so distant.

She hadn't imagined they would be enforced.

But now she was back. A reminder that she was part of a relatively old-fashioned system, and that she was the daughter of a king's advisor.

But what if you did walk away?

She would walk away with nothing. And she had no idea what she would do with that. What would she be able to offer…anyone? How would she take care of herself? The job that she had at a charity was fulfilling, but it didn't make a large amount. And she had always known that she would have an arranged marriage. It was just that…

It was just that she had wanted the marriage that was arranged.

"I can see it's going well."

She whirled around, and the book flew off of her head. And there he was. Standing in the door, the object of her consternation.

"Very well," she said dryly.

"Concentrating hard in your lessons?"

"Thinking about running away."

He began to move closer to her, and her heart beat faster in response. She didn't know why she found him so… So.

"There will be none of that," he said.

"Why?"

"You know what happens when people run into the woods."

But he was not teasing her. His voice was heavy.

"I'm not going to run into the woods."

"A relief. Good to know that you do have some sense in your head."

"I was actually beginning to wonder if I do. I could go back to America."

"You could," he said. "With nothing."

"I don't need a lot of money."

"But your charity…"

"Yes. It's an astronomical waste of privilege, isn't it."

"Interesting that you think that way. When it isn't as if you have a whole lot of choice."

"I don't. But I do have… I have benefited very much from all the money that has surrounded me my entire life. To completely disregard it seems short-sighted."

And she realized that she stood there, staring up

at him, that she also had no idea what her life looked like if she cut ties with Liri. With her homeland.

With this palace, and with this man.

No, she had never been close to Alex. But he had always been there. He had been there during her years at University, however distant.

It hadn't been her mother who had supported her then. But the palace.

Her mother had gone off to find a way to keep herself in the lifestyle she was accustomed to, at least from Tinley's point of view. She'd found lovers who aided in that pursuit.

She'd told Tinley she couldn't understand why she didn't find a rich husband.

Why she needed school.

Why she needed to make her own life.

Even being responsible and independent, Tinley was wrong.

The palace was the reason she had the cottage. She doubted Alex had overseen any of it personally, but her connections to the royal family had been a safety net for her.

And even now, this palace—though she had avoided it for many years now—was a particular sort of safety net. And she supposed that in some ways going along with all this was a bit of cowardice. But she couldn't... Couldn't fathom simply deciding to cut herself off from this. Her final connection to her father. Her final connection to the life she'd been meant to have.

She had a chance here, to have a say in her future.

And no, not in the way other women did, it was true. But she could choose her husband. She could find someone who did suit her.

It was archaic in some ways, she knew. Or it would seem so to other people. But she'd had a husband chosen for her as a girl. To have an actual selection now seemed nearly decadent.

And marriage… This was the key to her succeeding, she knew it was.

She'd given up pleasing her mother.

But she could *show* her.

With the right husband she would have the assets she needed to make a difference in the world. The right husband would like her as she was. And she could show her mother that she could make a success of herself.

That she didn't need to be a queen or even a princess.

"I don't need to be turned into a robot. I want whoever I marry to marry *me*, not some elegant lie." she said. "This is ridiculous."

"Now," he said, his voice stern. "That isn't terribly polite, considering Madame Dansforth makes a living at this ridiculousness. It is her life's work."

Tinley turned to her instructor. "I didn't mean your life's work is ridiculous." She turned back to Alex. "What I meant is it's ridiculous to try to make me into something I'm not. I'm never going to be able to maintain anything like this." She held her foot out, displaying the impractical high heel she was wearing. "I'm not going to be swanning around my house wearing things like this. So if I managed to impress a man, it's going to be based on nothing but a lie that I will never be able to keep up for more than a few hours."

"Best foot forward."

She wiggled her toes. "Clumsy foot."

She hated this. Because it reminded her so much of what it was like to be a clumsy, sad girl who couldn't do anything right as far as her mother was concerned.

She took in a long, slow breath. And it caught, somewhere in the center of her chest, as her eyes met his.

"I am supposed to find a husband for you," he said. "And I will do it by the means that I consider to be best."

"And you never question your opinions?"

"I question them often," he said. "Any leader should." And she felt something bloom there at the center of her chest. Hot and reckless and strange. Irritation. Because it could be nothing more.

Because she resented him. Resented him, and the fact that he lived and breathed and stood there disapproving of her while his brother was gone.

That he had taken her here and manipulated the connection she still had to this family, to this place, against her.

That isn't fair. You chose this. You chose this because you're afraid to do anything else. Because you want to show your mother...

She shut that thought down.

Along with the reckless heat inside of her.

"How is dancing coming along?" he asked, not directing the question to her at all.

"We haven't begun," Madame Dansforth said.

"Then we will begin now."

"The girl has not managed to walk across the room with the book on her head," the madam snapped.

"Will she be walking across the ballroom with a book on her head?" Alex asked, his tone dry. "Because she will be dancing. So it is perhaps in her best interest if she practices one above the other."

Madame Dansforth looked exasperated. "I have a method, and you did hire me to use it."

"Yes," he said. "But I'm still the King. And I'm overriding you now."

There was a pause and if Tinley wasn't mistaken, a hint of frost in the air. But the good madam knew better than to argue with a king.

"As you wish, Your Majesty," the woman said.

It really was amazing how people deferred to him, even if they were irritated, as Madame Dansforth visibly was. It was only that no one dared say it to his face. That he was being high-handed. That he was overstepping. When he so clearly was.

When the music started, Alex turned to her.

"Dance," he said. He extended his hand, and she looked at it, having the feeling that he had offered her a live spider.

"With you?"

"Yes," he said. "I will be dancing with you the night of the ball. It is my job to present you."

"That seems a little bit much."

"It's a dance," he said. "Not a siege against your person."

But for some reason, as she reached out to take his hand, slowly, ever so slowly, she felt as if they might be the same thing.

She thought of another moment. Another time.

She'd been nearly eighteen and standing against the wall during a ball. Dionysus had danced with two other women then slipped off to get drunk. She felt numb and she'd tried to tell herself it was only that he hadn't known how she felt. That their relationship had not yet become a romantic one, not for him. Still, it had hurt.

She hadn't known quite what to do with herself and Alexius had come over to her, dark eyes alight with black fire.

We will dance.

Oh, no I'm fine.

It wasn't a request.

And she'd found herself swept up into strong arms that had made her feel small, fragile and safe, all at once.

His hand on her waist had burned and she'd been able to think of nothing else the whole time he'd twirled her around the dance floor. She'd been holding her breath and the relief she'd felt when he'd released her had been beyond words.

Because she hated him.

Because he hadn't done it for any reason other

than because he was Alex, and when it came to duty he'd do it whether he wanted to or not.

But in the present, when their fingers connected, something shot through her midsection, down between her thighs.

And it made her wonder if what she'd felt back then had been hate at all.

It reminded her of a time she had gone on a hike when she'd been at college. They had gone up to the very top of a ridge, and she had stood on the edge, looking down, and she felt it. That kind of terror. That resonated in her core. In her teeth.

Fear. That's what this was. She feared him.

The Lion of the Dark Wood.

Except, to her, he would always be entangled in the wolves that had eaten his brother.

Somehow, to her, they had become one in the same. This forbidding older brother whose job it was to protect an entire country, but somehow hadn't protected his blood.

He had become the villain of the story. And she couldn't quite figure out why. Because of course it wasn't his responsibility to monitor every movement of his younger brother. It was even more ridiculous than the blame he took from the public, for being a boy, a small boy, who had failed to supervise another child. There should have been nannies. There should have been guards. His parents. Why was Alex the one who seemed to take the unequal weight in all of this?

And yet, she tended to think of him in that way

as well. As the responsible party for something that had gone wrong.

And maybe it was because of everything that had come before, more than legends and curses. Because in her memory, the palace had been wonderful. And Dionysus had been wonderful. But Alex had never approved, and it had been transparent, at least to her.

Alex had always felt like their villain.

He had that way of stealing her rose colored glasses.

It made her feel raw and wounded and fragile. Because her advocates were gone. And it was he who remained.

And then, it wasn't only her fingertips that touched his. His large hand enveloped hers, and he pulled her against his body. She stumbled in the high heels, falling against that hard, broad chest. With her free hand, she braced herself, and then removed it as if she had been scalded.

"Dance," he repeated.

Then he swept her into his arms, and he took the lead.

He was strong, and steady, but her heart was beating at some erratic, ridiculous clip, and she could not manage to keep her feet beneath her. She kept slipping, tripping, trembling.

Madame Dansforth was shouting out instructions, and Tinley could feel herself failing. Alarmingly off rhythm.

She hated it. Hated this. It reminded her of being at home. Her mother had tried to get her dancing lessons and she'd failed. She'd been awful at piano. Her mother had placed coins on the backs of her hands to get her to play with her hands held just so, and they'd always clattered onto the floor. She'd had her sit in a dining chair with a scarf tied around her shoulders to improve her posture.

Even dinner had to be a lesson, because she couldn't even eat right.

She couldn't do this right, and Alex's disapproval burned even deeper.

"Leave us," Alex shouted.

They stopped moving, and his voice echoed over the music. Madame Dansforth looked at him, her expression blank. "Leave you?"

"I do not think my order was ambiguous."

The woman paused. "Of course it wasn't."

"Good."

She left them, leaving them alone. And Tinley simply stood, standing in front of Alex, feeling small and inadequate and *angry*.

"Dance again," he commanded.

"You've dismissed the instructor."

"She wasn't helping you. I am your instructor now."

"You don't know that she wasn't helping. You don't know me."

"I do know you," he said. "You are the girl that my father matched up with my brother simply because he thought the world of your father. It had nothing to do with you. It had nothing to do with him."

"How dare you?"

"It is the truth," he said. "I'm sorry if you find it inconvenient."

"I didn't ask for this. Not any of it."

"And yet, there are hoops we all must jump through in order to fulfill our destinies, are there not? What is my life but a public performance? But a show. And it is not the most important thing that I am. For a show will not run a country. I must do that. I must keep the people secure. Keep them safe. I must fulfill the destiny of the nation. I must do it while instilling confidence in myself as a leader."

"Difficult to do. You're a walking PR problem."

He smiled. A predator's smile.

Lion or wolf, it didn't matter.

It was still all the better to eat her with.

"Dance."

"On my terms." She kicked her shoes off, which was not the power move she had hoped, since that put her directly in the line of sight of the center of his chest. And then, in a state of rage, she grabbed hold of the band that held her hair in place, and pulled it free. "Now I'll dance. As me. Not as this…trussed up turkey on stilts."

She found herself back in his arms, and this time, when he began to lead, his strong arms nearly lifted her off the ground.

They moved in time with the music. Rough. Angry. Intense. But she didn't feel off rhythm now. For she moved with him. As if their rage had twined together, flowing through them both.

Her every move was now in time with his. Her

heart thundered, her body quaking as they did. She had never been this close to a man before. She had danced light and carefree at parties. The way that young people did. Holding hands, and not inviting any intimacy.

She had danced with Dionysus and he had kept that sort of distance. Out of deference to her father and her age.

He had treated her as a perfect gentleman.

And Alexius was as well. He certainly wasn't taking liberties. It was simply a dance. But her breasts were crushed against his chest, and it felt like a sin. And the most disturbing thing was she had a feeling that sensation of sinning came from inside her own body. And the expression on his face sharpened, turned to stone.

It wasn't disapproving anymore.

It was something else. Something she couldn't pin a name on. But it echoed inside of her. She knew, somehow, that it matched. That it matched the reckless feeling that was riding through her like a rhythm all its own. One that overrode the music. One that sounded a call to a different kind of dance.

You know.

Something inside of her whispered that. From a place deep and hidden.

And she felt horribly exposed. Bright and sensitive, and like exactly what he thought she was. Something untamed and coarse and unworthy.

A woman who had kicked her shoes off in his presence, and unbound her hair.

And yet, he held her. Yet, he didn't let her go. It was an anomaly. One she could not put a name to. They twirled around the ballroom floor, and while the thick, leaden sensation that was so foreign to her pooled in her stomach, created alchemy and heat inside of her, she didn't notice she had been lifted off the floor. That she was spun so her back pressed against the wall, and even more hard and unyielding than the marble behind her, was the man at her front.

His dark eyes blazed down into hers, and she lost the ability to breathe.

But he didn't move. A sense of wretched desperation filled her. But it could not be. It could not be that this quickening of her heart, that the sensitivity she felt in her breasts, down between her legs was anything like desire.

Desire for this man who was wrapped in the most painful memories she possessed.

The brother of the man she'd been so certain she loved.

And he wouldn't answer the question of what this dark, terrible beast inside her wanted. He wouldn't do anything to ease her suffering.

Had he moved away from her, or had he closed the distance, she might have found some clarity. But he refused to do either. He held them both there, frozen, poised as if on the edge of a knife.

"Learn to dance in shoes," he said finally. And then he moved away from her.

And he left her feeling...cold. Bereft of something that she would have denied she wanted unto death.

And she was helpless to do anything but stare as she watched him walk out of the ballroom.

She leaned against the wall, collapsed, sliding down to the floor. And she stared at the book she had been balancing on her head only moments ago, lying in the center of the room discarded.

What had she done? Or worse still, what hadn't she done, that a piece of her seemed to want.

"This is the problem," she whispered. "Yarn and cats can only take you so far. And loving a dead man doesn't do much for pent up physical desire."

She had always thought that maybe… That maybe her desire was low. That maybe she didn't have all that much. She had found Dionysus beautiful, but she had been young.

She hadn't had…fantasies about him.

But she had felt comfortable with him, and she had liked him. She'd told herself that made their feelings pure, for it wasn't clouded by anything base.

She hadn't felt that great weight of discomfort in his presence like she had done with Alexius. But tonight that discomfort had twisted into something else, and she despised it.

She despised herself.

She needed to untangle it, but she didn't want to.

And the truly terrible thing was that she was quite stuck with the man for a bit of time yet.

"It's nothing," she whispered.

And she whispered it again when she was shut up in her room, lying on the bed and scratching Algernon behind the ears.

Restlessness rolled through her. She got up off the bed and walked over to her little pet cages. Offering both Peregrine and the hedgehogs a treat. She felt a deep, enduring sadness. And she couldn't pinpoint quite why.

It was an ache that started around her heart and spread, affecting her breathing.

You're lonely.

She was. Lonely and a coward, and it was all kind of sad.

If she left here…if she left Alex…

The idea made her feel devastated and she didn't know why.

"But if I get married, I won't be lonely," she whispered into the room.

Except she knew that wasn't necessarily true. And the weight of that truth filled her with a sadness so profound she found it difficult to breathe past it.

CHAPTER FIVE

ALEXIUS WAS IN his office the next day when she appeared unannounced.

The sight of her was like a physical punch straight to his gut.

She wasn't dressed up. She had no makeup on, her freckles in full view. She had on a pair of jeans, and a soft-looking T-shirt that molded itself to her full breasts. Her hair was in a state, and he found himself wishing he could sink his fingers deep into those tresses.

He gritted his teeth. He had very nearly made a mistake with her when they had danced in the ballroom.

He was not accustomed to this. To this feeling.

The sort of reckless, out-of-control sensation.

Temptation.

In his world there was no temptation.

He did not act in a way that might endanger Liri, and if he did want something, and it did not endanger the future of his country, then he set about getting it.

He was a man who conducted his business in matter-of-fact ways.

But Tinley lived in an astonishing gray area.

Having her would cause an endless stream of problems. An array of issues that would echo throughout his life. The first issue being that her father would likely come back from the dead and haunt him. The second being... He could not marry her. Neither did he want to. He had arrangements made. She had been his brother's fiancée, and the optics of taking her as a wife...

The entire country had perceived the match between Tinley and Dionysus as a love match. To take his dead brother's future wife, particularly when his own failures were mixed in to the cause of his brother's demise...

No matter what he thought about her ability to fulfill the role as Queen, it was something that simply could not be borne.

And there would be no touching her without a commitment.

Except you could. She wants you. You could, and no one would know.

No. Only his conscience. Only his honor.

Walking that line was why he remained.

And he would continue to walk it still.

Atonement for past sins that could never truly be forgiven.

"What is it you want?" he asked.

"I want to discuss the logistics of this ball."

"There is nothing to discuss. It will happen. A husband for you will be found."

"Who is doing the choosing?"

Frustration shot through him like an arrow.

"I feel it will be apparent who is right for you when you're both in the same room."

"Are you playing Cupid?"

"Nothing of the kind."

"Do I get to choose?"

"You get to choose," he said. "I'm certainly not frog-marching you down the aisle."

A thoughtful expression crossed her face. "And who will be in attendance? Will there be anyone I can look at beforehand?"

"You make it sound as if you're buying a used car."

"Well, it seems only right that I be able to kick the tires of my future husband."

"Certainly," he said. And then he realized that he had not personally overseen any of the guest list. He had handed it off, as was his typical practice when he felt a deep aversion to something.

And he shouldn't.

You don't want to share.

"Well, tell me about them."

"Of course."

He pulled out a file for the event, and perused the guest list. He found he did know a few of them.

"Robert Martin," he said. "He's an American philanthropist. Very wealthy. You'll like him."

"How old is he?"

"Near my age, I believe."

"Does he have all his teeth?"

"I've never asked."

"Who else?"

"Marcus Weber. He's British. Descendent of some minor nobility or another. An innovator in green technologies."

"Well, I like the sound of both of them."

"So there. You will be quite happy."

"When am I expected to make a decision?" She asked. "Do I have until midnight on my birthday?"

"Tinley," he said. "It is not so easy."

"You're the one who came in issuing commands. I want a timeline. Don't you have…a way that you think this will work?"

"We will evaluate after the ball."

"You're very cavalier with my life."

"I'm not being cavalier. I can assure you that I never have been, not for one moment. You have me confused with someone else." He let the words settle between them.

"No," she said softly. "I would never confuse the two of you." She began to move away from his desk, and then she stopped. "You're a king. You're kind of…all-powerful. You don't know what it's like to have this much of your freedom tied up. I can leave, but I'll leave with nothing. You don't have any clue what that's like."

She had no idea. None at all. He'd had to live under the shadow of two deaths. He'd had to hold himself back when he'd wanted nothing more than to destroy the agreements made between their families.

She knew nothing about his life.

About the curse he lived under.

"I know all about not having freedom," he said, rage pouring through him. "Do you think that if left to my own devices I would've chosen to live as I did? Of course not. I was born a man like any other, but I must be a king instead. Do you not think I would've enjoyed womanizing and drinking as my brother did? Perhaps I would have. But I had to be strong. I had to be a symbol, not a human being, and I continue to act in that way. Do you think that I'm choosing my own wife now? For sentimental reasons? Or even for the reason of desire?" He stood, and rounded the desk, which he knew was a mistake, even as he did it.

He knew it was a mistake. A dark thrill worked its way through his body. For he did not make mistakes. But he made this one, and deliberately. Because the word *desire* arced between them like an electric current, and he could feel it, resonating down below his belt. Throbbing there.

He had sex. And plenty of it. With women who were willing. With women who knew the score, absolutely and completely. All of his decisions about sex were made clearly and consciously. He did not act on impulse.

The first time he had realized he wanted to deviate from that had been when he had cornered Tinley in the corridor of the palace once, at barely eighteen. When that initial kick of desire he'd tried to push off

as an aberration when he'd seen her in her swimsuit
had turned into something darker, sharper.

Something he couldn't ignore.

She and his brother had caused some sort of spectacle at a state dinner, and he had felt compelled
to scold them both. But her before Dionysus, and
he hadn't immediately known why. But he had followed her, that trail of red hair and humor, down
the hall from the dining room, and when she had
turned and looked up at him, those eyes had been
wide. And then she had licked her lips and he had
felt it like a glide of her tongue against his manhood.
And he had known then. What forbidden was. What
desire was. And why those two things together created something delicious that he would never be able
to explore.

His brother was a known womanizer, so even
then, he doubted that Tinley was a virgin. Would it
be so bad then for him to touch her?

He had entertained that, if only for a moment.

For virgin or not, she was his brother's. If he'd decided that he wanted her, and then desired to return
her to Dionysus, he would be within his right to do
so. He was the King. The future King. And no one
could tell him he could not. His weight and rank far
outstripped his brother. And there was nothing his
brother had that he could not.

He knew the true temptation of an abuse of power
then as well.

And none of it would have been half so dangerous if he hadn't seen a strange, innocent desire in her

eyes too. The sort of desire he imagined she didn't quite understand.

But with the right touch, the right kiss, she would have.

And that was when he took a step back. Because he was pondering violating everything that he was supposed to be for the chance to touch a woman who was unsuitable. A woman who should not possess the ability to tempt him. And she tempted him now. Still. Four years later.

A glaring testament to the weakness that lived inside of him.

To the dark terror he truly suspected. That the world was random and he was the lion of nothing. Not chosen for any one particular thing. Just alive.

A man who had let his brother wander into the woods so he could have a taste of what his brother had. Who perhaps had wanted to ensure that he could never be challenged by this spare who had no true responsibilities. And who had a woman that made Alex's heart beat faster and his blood run hotter.

She reminded him of all those things, of all those potential shortcomings, even now. And it ate at him like acid in his gut.

But worse, the look on her face set a fire to his blood, made it flow hot and fast and low, pooling below his belt. Making him hard.

"I'm engaged," he said.

"You are?" The question came out a hoarse whisper.

"Perhaps not in the way you might think of it. But

I'm in the process of drawing up an agreement with an Arabian socialite. Nadia is exactly what I want in a queen. She is everything suitable to this position. The position of Queen. And that is why I have chosen her."

"I…"

"You must marry in your twenty-third year. I must marry by my thirty-fifth. And so, we are both in the middle of the deadline, you see."

"And you just chose someone. Just like that?"

"Yes."

"What about love?"

"What about it?"

"Did your parents love each other?"

"I don't know. I never asked."

"I didn't have to ask mine. They didn't. And it made the lives of everyone around them quite miserable."

"No one is around me."

The truth of his own words struck him then.

"What are you talking about? You have an entire household of people around you."

"It is not the same. We are separate. By station."

"And when you have children?"

He did not like to think of such things, nor of the future. Living here in this palace on the edge of a forest that had consumed so much. But it would be different. He would be different. "We will have nannies. Guards."

"And you won't do any parenting?"

"It won't be necessary. I am King, and I will protect."

She reached out, and her fingertips made contact with his suit jacket sleeve.

He shrugged her off. "Do not test me, Tinley."

"What would I be testing?" She took a step toward him, and the expression on her face reminded him so much of when he had caught her out in the corridor four years ago.

Hours before his brother's death.

"If you don't know," he growled. "Then you should truly think before you put a hand on me."

"Why have you always hated me? I know you never thought I was worthy of him."

"I don't hate you. It would be simpler to hate you. And as for worthiness? It is not as simple as that."

"What is it then?"

"You stand out. That is not in the job description for a princess."

"That will always be the issue, won't it? My standing out. I'm sorry that I was born objectionable. But your brother did not seem to find me objectionable at all."

Rage poured through him. At him, at her. At Dionysus. At everything. He hated it. For it was grandly out of control, because it made him like her. And he was different. He had to be different. For the weight of the crown rested on his shoulders.

And the minute he took his focus away from what mattered, everything could be so easily destroyed.

But his focus was off everything but her. Everything but those glimmering green eyes, and everything that seemed to shimmer beneath the surface of her skin. Everything he wondered about, but had taken steps not to.

She haunted him.

And he mourned his brother, but he saw him for who he was. She still defended him. Above Alex.

As everyone did.

"My brother found every woman who would warm his bed acceptable. And believe me when I tell you he had counted on a life where he could have you and whoever else he fancied. Do not think my brother was going to promise you fidelity. Do not think that you were some great love of his. It is a shame that you build your life as a monument to him when he would never have done the same for you."

"You don't know," she said, color rising in her face. "He was my friend."

"Friendship does not keep a spark alive in the marriage bed."

"And you speak with such great authority on marriage? On relationships? You're brokering a business deal for your own."

He scoffed. "What makes you think yours was any different? Business between our fathers. A reward for time spent serving in my father's court. Your mother might have found you unsuitable, but your father found you an easy pawn."

"He didn't," she said. "He loved me." Her voice faltered there.

"There is no question he did, Tinley, but he was

a man. Flesh and blood mortal. And we all of us are subject to the weakness inherent in that state. And perhaps in part for all that he could gain from having a daughter. Most men would want a son, but not a man with the ear of the King. For his daughter could marry into our family."

"Even if that played a role in my relationship with my father," she said, her tone dripping with disdain as she took a step toward him. "It is no different than you. Your father had three sons. An heir and two spares. How lucky for him. Except your family is cursed. Strife between brothers or death. You're no less an accident of birth than I am."

"An accident of death spared you." He reached out and grabbed hold of her chin. Her skin was impossibly soft beneath his own, and it reminded him of yesterday's dance. Yesterday's failure. "For you would have wasted away here. Bored. Your bed empty while your husband went and amused himself elsewhere. You could have become a jaded courtier. Entertaining extra lovers as you saw fit while the staff raised your children."

He had let himself think, for years, she might have been happy with Dionysus. But he'd been lying to himself. Not Tinley. Tinley would never have sat back and been contented with that life, not forever.

He'd thought because of how she'd been during their engagement she might be.

But she'd been young. That was all.

And now...now less so.

"Why are you like this?" Her eyes glittered, not

with anger, with unshed tears, and it was that show of emotion that saw him dropping his hand to his side and taking a step away.

"You have to believe it, don't you? You have to believe all those things about him. Otherwise you might feel truly guilty for the fact you didn't protect the remaining son your parents had that wasn't you. That wasn't anything more than an icon of the crown. Dionysus was a person. You're… You're not a man. You're a beast. At best. A rock at worst. Stone. Unfeeling and cruel. You have to believe Dionysus would have disappointed me because otherwise you don't know how you live with the guilt. It doesn't matter if he could have been responsible for his actions. You're the King. Even if you weren't on the throne then, you always had that power in you. You should have stopped him. You were his older brother and you didn't. You had the power to remove me from my home and bring me here. To demand that I marry. You had the power to stop him that night. To stop himself from making a fool of the family and wandering into his certain death. You certainly could've stopped him from having another woman at the party. But you didn't want to, because you didn't want me with him anyway. Is that the truth of it? That you liked him parading that other girl around on his arm? Because you knew it might get back to me?"

"I didn't think it would hurt you to know the truth."

Her words cut deep, because there was a truth to

them. His brother had been more and more careless with his whoring. And there was a time when it had mattered little, because Tinley was young and he wasn't going to be in an intimate relationship with someone her age. But they were at the point where their marriage would have been coming soon, and the engagement had been officially announced. And that meant there was no excuse for him appearing in public with other women.

The fact was she wasn't wrong about any of it.

He had been angry with Dionysus and he had been happy to allow his brother to make a fool of himself so that he actually had a mess to clean up.

He had been happy to give himself a moment to indulge himself in what he wanted most of all.

Dionysus had female company for the evening, and it wasn't Tinley so why shouldn't Alex have…

And had it gone that way, he would feel no guilt. But the consequences for allowing him to go off on his drunken night had been permanent and irreversible. He was only grateful the woman who had been with Dionysus had not been an unintended casualty. She had been traumatized, certainly. But not harmed.

"If you consider it my job as King to conceal people from the truth, then you're correct," he said, his voice stone. "I was lax in my duties. I thought he was your friend. I thought you knew him. You certainly weren't my friend."

The truth of it resonated between them. They'd known each other years, and they were not friends.

They never would be.

"I wouldn't be surprised if you didn't have any friends."

"Kings don't have them."

"Your father did. So I suppose that's just a lie you tell yourself to feel better about living here. By yourself. With no one. At least, no one who likes you." She turned to leave and that same recklessness that was only ever present when Tinley was near fired through him. He reached out and grabbed her arm, stopped her from leaving. She turned around, her eyes wide, her lips parted softly. He could see her breath coming shorter, harder. Faster.

"You might not like me," he said, his voice like gravel. A stranger's voice. "But you feel something else, something more than hate, and I think you find it disturbing."

"What do you think I feel?"

He reached out and touched a lock of that unruly hair, and the fire inside of him nearly exploded. But outwardly, he kept himself still. She was frozen, like a startled doe caught in the headlights. The pulse of the base of her throat beat rapidly. He moved his hand, cupping her face, sliding his thumb along her cheekbone, then tracing the line of her lower lip.

She was so soft. Impossibly so.

The beach.

The ballroom.

The corridor.

It all burned between them now.

Those moments filled with anger and recrimination and resistance.

"You're not so naïve that you don't know what this means."

His words broke the spell, and she jerked away from him.

"Nothing," she said. "I find you disgusting."

"So disgusting that your heart is beating fast, and your pupils have dilated so that your eyes are nearly black."

"Fear," she said, her voice breathless.

"You don't fear me. You should. But you don't. Perhaps that's the problem, Tinley. You're a woman who wants a challenge. I'm the biggest challenge around. Perhaps what you really want is to test your strength against mine."

"There's no way I could fight you. You would destroy me."

"I don't mean a fight. Perhaps you wish to test your strength against mine. In a bed."

He could see the moment he had pushed her too far, and he realized he had been trying for just that. Because if she took one step toward him they were both lost. So he had no choice but to try and force her into taking a step away.

"Why would I want that?"

"I've heard that sex often holds more appeal when the object of desire is forbidden." And then she did something he did not expect. She turned and she ran. She left his office door wide open as she did, not even taking the time to close it behind her.

He had done it. He had pushed her away. And he supposed he should feel some triumph in that.

Instead he just felt the ache in his gut widened.
He had won nothing.

And for a man in his position, it was unacceptable.

But he had been unacceptable for a very long
time. Without even a hint of satisfaction to make
it bearable.

CHAPTER SIX

SHE STOOD THERE on the edge of the wood.

The Dark Wood.

Her cottage was on the other side of it. And she knew there was no way she could ever pass through and make it out alive.

But as she stared into the dense green wildness, she wondered if this was what had driven Prince Lazarus forward when he'd been a boy. She wondered if even drunk, this is what Dionysus had felt the need to test himself against.

This deep, dark forest filled with secrets. Filled with danger.

It was a mystery.

She wondered, sometimes, why the royal family had not cleared the wood. Knocked it over.

But there was now, and had always been, such a strange relationship with the royal family and this enchanted place. They had won wars there, bolstered against their enemies by their knowledge of the forest. They had lost kings, sons, daughters to the dangers of the wood. Generationally. It was as if the source of their power came from it, as well as the source of their potential demise.

And what of her own demise? It seemed to be back there in the palace.

He'd said all those things to her, and they had cut her deeply. His words were sharp knives, and she had felt the cut of every single one of them. And then he had touched her. And his skin was so warm and enticing. A temptation, even as his words caused harm.

He'd spoken to her of dark things that she barely understood.

And she had felt no less like she was standing on the edge of a perilous wood in his office then she did now. In fact, the Dark Wood seemed safer.

For Alexius contained mysteries. She suspected there was a dark magic beneath his tailored suits. Shattered things brought to light resting in the palm of his hand. If he touched her, would he light up all those things that were still hidden from her?

When he touched her, she felt bright.

Even as anger simmered through her blood, there was something else that he had ignited over the surface of her skin.

I've heard that sex often holds more appeal when the object of desire is forbidden.

Her breath caught.

She wasn't running from him. She was running from herself. Perhaps that was what brought everyone to the edge of this wood. Fleeing yourself.

For that's what it had to be. You had to be more frightened of the monsters outside of it, than the monsters that might be within. Otherwise... You would never set foot in it.

"What are you doing?"

She whirled around to see a mountain of large, angry alpha male coming her way. His expression was thunderous, filled with rage.

"Nothing," she said.

"Get away from there." He closed the distance between them and grabbed hold of her, physically moving her a foot away from where she had been standing. "Don't be a fool."

"I'm not being a fool. Running away from you is the first sensible thing I've done in days."

"And so you would run into the wood? You would never come back out."

"You think you can survive the wood, but I can't?"

"You think Lazarus and Dionysus can perish there but not you?"

"I guess my arrogance matches yours."

"Do not be a fool," he said again, his words carrying a veil of threat over them.

"If I'm a fool it's because you chased me away. Perhaps you should reflect on that."

It was a lie. And she spoke those words with no conviction, and she knew that he heard it.

"I think," he said, his voice soft and deadly, "*cara mia*, that you were running away from yourself."

And that was when she found herself being hauled toward him, and when his lips crashed down on hers it was like the whole mountain had fallen over the top of her.

His mouth was hot and firm and certain as it moved over hers. And she… She was lost.

She had shared pleasant, nice kisses with Dionysus that had felt nothing like being wrapped up in fire.

But that's what this was. Licks of flame moving over her skin as he parted her lips and licked into her mouth.

She had never seen the attraction to kissing like this.

With all of yourself.

With the full weight of your body pressed against another person, and your lips parted, gaining them access to taste you. She had never understood why the scrape of someone's teeth against her lips might be erotic. But it was. Everything about this was. And she realized then that she should have just gone straight into the Dark Wood, for she had a better chance of emerging unscathed than she did from this kiss.

But he was uncompromising.

He did not allow her to rethink. Not because he was holding her with his strength, but because he immobilized her, in thrall because of his mastery of her body.

She was cocooned in his arms. He was so big and hard and he lifted her up from the ground with no effort at all. One large palm was pressed between her shoulder blades, the other low on her back. And he kissed her. Like a beast.

Like a wolf.

Set on devouring her.

She couldn't breathe. She was dizzy with it. With the slick glide of his tongue against hers and the heavy strength of his hands weighting her to the earth.

For if he wasn't holding her she was sure she would fly apart into a million pieces and be lost as a mist in the air. There was salvation in this devouring, and she could not explain it any more than she could understand it. But she could feel it.

Oh, she could feel it.

And then, as suddenly as he had caught her up, he set her back down onto the ground. The rejection was startling. Verging on terrifying. For somehow, the world had been tilted on its axis and she didn't know who she was when she wasn't in Alex's arms.

Alex.

Alex, who had always felt like a dark, forbidding figure in the corner of her world. But the lens had shifted now and he felt like the center of it. No less dark, no less forbidding. But more tempting than the wood itself.

"You," he said, his voice low. "You have tempted me for far too long. And it is unacceptable. I am not tempted. I do not deviate from the path."

He turned away from her then, and walked back toward the palace, leaving her standing there, shattered.

He had been tempted by her?

He had been tempted by her. Those words echoed inside of her like dark magic.

He had wanted her. All those years when he had been disapproving? She could remember when he had come after her one night, there had been a dinner party, and she and Dionysus had been laughing at the end of the table. She knew that Alex had disapproved of their behavior, found them disruptive. Treating them like naughty children rather than the young adults they'd been. She had been annoyed with him, as she always was. And her annoyance with Alex always felt large. It was never simple.

It always seemed to take up every available space inside of her, then expand.

There was something about Alex that always did that to her.

And she could remember him cornering her in a corridor, his dark eyes blazing with black fire.

That is not the behavior of a princess.

And is this but the behavior of a future king?

You should show me more respect.

You should give it.

Earn it. Though I would prefer you did it as an occasional houseguest, and not as the future wife of my brother.

Do you not wish to be my brother-in-law, Alex? Is our relationship quite so damaged?

She remembered how his irritation had flared up.

But something deeper. Something more.

And now she wondered.

She wondered now if the feeling inside of her whenever she had been alone with him had not been fear. Had not been irritation at his disapproval, but a desire to…

As he'd said. To test herself against him.

Because he wanted her.

And if he wanted her, in this state that he disapproved of so…

Didn't that make it powerful?

It was like the sun had risen on a personal darkness inside of her, and lit it all up.

She could not be controlled. Any more than her hair could be. She wasn't tamed.

And that was what her mother hated. It was what bothered Alex.

She was chaotic, it was true. And she could be messy. And most of all, she simply wasn't that which all the people around her seemed hell-bent on making her into.

And they couldn't force her to, not with the whole weight of their disapproval.

And Alex wanted her anyway.

He wanted to marry her off, he wanted to get rid of her.

He wanted to do his duty and not have to face this big, bright thing between them that was wrong in every single way.

Wrong.

Yes, it was wrong. That Alex had the power to ignite this thing in her blood that no other man had. Not even Dionysus, who she had been certain she loved.

Perhaps it was just age. Perhaps she was coming into herself a little later than some.

Maybe now any man would have the power to invoke this kind of response in her.

But she didn't think so.

Her body felt overly sensitive the entire day following the incident. And it was the eve of the ball, and a team of servants were sent to her room.

"You must be prepared," Charis said.

She was led to a place in the palace that she had never been before. Down a winding staircase, all the way down to the bottom of the palace, where she would have assumed that a dungeon might exist. But there was no dungeon here.

Instead, it was nothing but marble tiles, intricate mosaic inlaid into the floors. Jewels.

A spectacle unlike anything she had ever seen in Liri. The country tended to be more Spartan than this. Everything quite medieval, rather than ornate.

"What is this?" she asked one of the women.

"The baths. The royal family has a long tradition of preparing for either war or celebration in the private baths."

Tinley had never heard of such a thing. It seemed rather a luxury for the royal family, as she knew them. For with the exception of Dionysus, they had been austere, not given to indulgence.

"There are several rooms," Charis told her.

"How will I know what to do?"

"I can stay and guide you if you like."

The thought of being assisted with bathing made Tinley uncomfortable. "No."

"I thought not. The first is cold. It will bring the blood closer to the surface of your skin. You can move through it quickly. Then there is a tub that's very hot, you go into that next. And finally, you'll find the perfumed pool. It has been prepared with essential oils to perfume your skin. There will be sugar scrubs and other products to make your skin glow. It is how the Queen always prepared for parties."

"Really?"

"Yes."

"Why is this so secret?"

"I think rather it's…humanizing. And the royal family always does resist being seen as human."

A very insightful comment, Tinley thought. For it was true. They were a lineage wrapped in legends that had survived centuries, and they seemed to do nothing to try and dispel it. "How long have you worked for them?"

Charis frowned. "Ten years. I remember you. As a girl. Just like I remember Dionysus. And the Queen." There was something in the way she said *the Queen* that stuck out to Tinley and she couldn't quite place it.

"Did you like him? Dionysus. Only, sometimes I don't think his brother did."

"Alex loved his brother very much," the woman said. "I think he doesn't know how to show it."

"Oh. That being human again."

She laughed. "Yes. I think of all of them, he resists it most of all."

Tinley was bundled into a robe, her clothes taken from her, and then she was sent into a small room with glimmering, clear gemstones on the wall. They reflected in the water, made it look like ice. Which was appropriate, because when Tinley slipped her robe off and got into the water, she was certain that her skin would not survive. It was freezing. She moved through the pool quickly, getting out on the other side. Her robe was back where she had entered, but it was too late to do anything about that.

Her skin burned, and felt bright. Tingling from the water. She couldn't tell if her blood felt closer to the surface of the skin, or if it had frozen right in her veins. She passed through to the next room, which had red gems inlaid, glittering on the walls like fire. And so, she didn't have to guess what she would feel like when she entered and exited this pool.

The scalding heat of the water was nearly unbearable, particularly after her ice bath, and Tinley was wondering if the royal family was human after all. She moved through that pool quickly as well.

After that, there came a long corridor. The rock laid into the wall was blue and jade, like swirling waves all around her. She walked on a narrow path, with water on either side of it, as if a river flowed underground here. It made shifting, moving reflections on the wall. There were pedestals on either side of her at the center of the corridor. In one bowl, there was a textured looking substance. She put her fingers in it, and found it was the sugar scrub Charis had spoken of.

There was a smaller bowl next to it, and she put a small measure of it inside. Then she smelled it.

It smelled… It was not floral, nor was it feminine. There was a rich, spicy scent to it, and she realized it reminded her of Alex.

Unbidden, she had an image of him walking through here, naked. Of him scrubbing this onto his skin, for he must.

In the bowl on the other side was a cream, and she took a small measure of that as well.

Then she continued on her way, walking naked through the hall.

She didn't know what she expected of the grand pool she'd been instructed was waiting for her, but it was… Something else entirely. It was not a large rectangle, no, rather it was a winding, organic looking body of water that extended around the corner she could not see. The entrance had a slow slope into deeper water, like the ocean, but here, the sand was made from marble, precious stones and gold.

It illuminated the water from beneath, and overhead, the glittering stones cast fractured light all around.

It was like being in a sparkling cave of gems, in a river of light. She stepped into the water slowly and sighed when she found the temperature perfect. She set her bowls down on the edge of the winding pool, and slid beneath the surface. She allowed the silence to envelop her. The solitude. These last days had been… She could not recognize her life. Or rather, she could, but it was a strange, twisted mirror, showing her the past while driving her on toward a future she could not envision.

Was she really going to marry a stranger? Was she truly going to meet that man tomorrow, choose him, and…have Alex arrange it?

Alex.

The mention of his name made her skin burn hot and bright and it had nothing to do with the water.

She came up for air, no longer feeling cocooned by the water.

She swam over to the edge of the pool and put a bit of the sugar scrub on her fingertips, working it over her body, grimacing at the roughness.

But part of her welcomed it. For it felt a bit like a punishment, and she was angry with her skin.

Her breasts.

That treacherous place between her thighs that she had never given much thought to until *him*.

Her heart, which was filled with fear and trepidation. Which lacked the courage to run away, but also the courage to embrace where she was with any full passion.

The heart stuck in limbo.

And had it not been for years now?

She had been certain of a path, and then it had vanished, and she had tried to find something new.

And instead hadn't she just sunk into some kind of strange rebellion at her mother.

Choosing to live in a tiny cottage and take a job

where she worked from home so she never had to concern herself with her image?

An image that felt so short of what she knew her mother wanted it to be.

So it was so much easier to pretend she didn't care.

And in many ways she didn't.

But part of her yearned for an acceptance she would never have.

And even now it made her chest ache.

But Alex wants you.

Even thinking it made her nipples go tight, even as she scrubbed that punishing mixture over her skin.

She finished quickly, touching herself only creating more problems. Then she submerged herself in the water again, rinsing it all away.

She swam forward, the warm water a pleasant glide now over her skin as she went. As she tried to school her mind into something blank.

The pool wound on, and she could sense the many feet of the palace above her, all stone and stark and intimidating. And now she would never not know that this was here underneath.

This enchanted river that was something so different than the enchanted wood that stood all around.

For this place did not offer certain death. But a strange kind of pleasure that seemed absent from everywhere else on these grounds.

She came around another bend, and stopped.

For there he was.

She knew it was him. It took only a glance for

her body to react in the most violent fashion. Her stomach seizing tight, her heart slamming against her breastbone. He was facing away from her, and he lifted his arms, running his fingers over his hair, water sluicing down his back. His every muscle moved and flexed as he did so. And she was enthralled.

His shoulders and back were so broad, his waist narrow. He was like a god.

Or a wolf.

The moment she had thought it might all be safe.

She had forgotten.

That the deadliest predator was in the palace walls, not beyond them.

She could slip away. She could. She should. But she was frozen.

Just as she had been on the edge of the Dark Wood.

So close to danger and unwilling to turn away from it.

Your heart lacks courage.

Her heart lacked courage and it was why she lived in a tiny cottage. Her heart lacked courage and it was why she was here. Moving toward a future that she wasn't sure she wanted.

It was why she had never gone to see her mother, not since college, and asked her why she never seemed to think she was enough. Not as a princess, not as a student, not as the head of a charity.

Why her hair was so wrong, and why her laugh

was so loud, and why everything she seemed to do held them at further and further distance.

She was suddenly so very tired of herself.

And whatever happened at the ball tomorrow night, it needed to happen because there was conviction in her heart, and not simply fear of what might happen if she didn't do as Alex bid her.

And she…

She wanted something. She wanted something she didn't have a name for. She wanted more of what he'd made her feel yesterday. Desired. For what she was. As she was before any makeovers or scrubs or whatever else was going to become of her before tomorrow night. All the comportment was certainly leading up to a fair amount of oil masks and waxed body parts and scrubbings and makeup.

And here she was, in this grand bath washed clean of anything. She had on no clothes, nothing that signified her as the former future Princess, the woman who had arrived at the palace in leggings. And he had on no suit. Nothing that made him King.

Except all the *everything* about him.

She was a virgin.

What had surprised her most about going to college was the fact that it wasn't all that rare. Even a lot of the boys she knew hadn't actually been with anyone yet. Though, by the end of the four years there, almost everyone had dealt with it. She was in the minority, but not alone, and none of her friends had ever mocked her for it. They had all known about Dionysus. And while they could certainly all relate to feeling awkward, or not finding the right person, the grief of losing someone they were in love with was unique to her, and as a result, no one had ever pressed her. But she knew plenty about sex.

She had one roommate in particular who had been quite active and comfortable with her sex drive, and she brought a fair amount of men back to the dorm. Her other roommate had been a bit more reserved, but by the end of school even she'd had a boyfriend who'd spent the majority of his nights there.

She also talked with enough of her friends about first times to know that while every experience was different there were certain things to expect.

And nerves was one of them. But they all survived it.

And maybe this was simply… This was right.

Maybe this was what the royal family owed her.

Because she had been bound up in them for so many years, and maybe… Maybe she would decide to marry no one. Maybe she would decide to walk away with nothing and no money.

And maybe that would mean never returning to this place, never being here where she had felt so accepted. Her father had been happy here, and that had spilled over to her. Dionysus had been kind. The King had treated her like another child.

But Alex, the man who had made her feel like she might not be enough, wanted her. And maybe that was the ending she needed. Maybe this was the courage her heart needed.

To be big and fierce and bold.

She wanted to be.

She played at it in her own little world. Rescuing animals and heading up a charity that spoke to something in her heart, and made everything she did feel natural. Doing the things that mattered to her without having to put herself out there. But she could certainly exploit her position as Dionysus's former fiancée. As the once-and-no-longer-future Princess of Liri.

Maybe she didn't need her family's money. Maybe she simply had to be bold enough to put herself forward.

Yes, she had rebelliously dug into her image, but she had still kept it to herself.

And perhaps the key to that lay on the other side of this mystery. On the other side of this man.

Dionysus had been a dynamic, and obvious, influence on her life. But Alex had always been there.

Alexius. Tall and broad and imposing and creating wide, sweeping feelings inside of her.

She had felt uncomfortable around him. Always. And when his lips had met hers yesterday she had to wonder exactly why.

If perhaps she didn't truly understand the real reason she felt uncomfortable around him.

If it had never actually been fear.

No. It was fear. And the fear heightened inside of her as she stepped toward him.

It was fear. But it was something else as well.

She had never felt afraid of Dionysus.

But she had never felt this mounting, terrible excitement either.

Alex had given her a deep, trembling excitement over the years that had frightened her unto her core.

She could remember being on the beach with him in Italy. Him being angry at her for her swimsuit...

It all came back in a rush. What the undercurrent of that anger was.

And she'd touched him...

This was like standing on the edge of a cliff and trying to bring herself to jump off of it. Having to trust that somehow the bottom didn't hold doom, but escape.

He turned suddenly. His dark eyes connected with hers, and she felt her nipples go tight. For she was exposed above the hips, hiding nothing from his sharp gaze.

And he was...

It was only a fleeting moment that she felt embarrassed over her own body, because then she was consumed with the look of his.

He was...

She had often thought of him as a mountain, and she was correct. His chest was broad and heavily muscled, covered with dark chest hair.

He was a man.

That word emblazoned itself on her mind, her soul.

He was not a boy. Not a young man her age. A man with strength and depth and vast experience. And he would not give quarter if she took a step toward him and then decided she was too frightened.

She knew. In that moment. She had to make a choice now, and there would be no reversing it. And so, with her heart pounding sickeningly in her ears, she took a single step toward Alexius. She took a single step toward courage.

CHAPTER SEVEN

SHE WAS A WITCH. There was no other explanation for it. He had been here in the baths, doing his best to scrub her from his skin, doing his best to scrub this unwanted desire from all that he was, and she had appeared. A siren in the water. Naked and glistening and far beyond the beauty he had ever allowed himself to imagine she might possess.

Her breasts were full and plump, rosy tipped and delicious.

Her waist nipped in gently, then sloped outward, rounding into luxurious hips that would be perfect for a man to hold on to. She was the embodiment of his temptation. Of his weakness. And when she took a step toward him, he knew that his fate was sealed.

He had spent much of his life denying a belief in fate.

For the legends about his family and fate were dark indeed, and they suggested that there was no hand stronger or mightier than that of an invisible, immovable force that might decide to rearrange the whole kingdom on a whim.

To kill young princes and leave but one remaining.

In his position, a belief in fate had always felt somewhat grim.

That he was chosen for some reason beyond anything he had done or could do. But his brothers had been chosen for death.

That belief did not make him stronger or better. That belief meant that trying was truly a pointless exercise. And so he had rejected it. But Tinley. Tinley had gotten under his skin for all these long years, and he had convinced himself that there was nothing in this world that was inevitable.

Here she was, a slick, bare inevitability that seemed to make a mockery of the idea that he could outrun anything. Her red hair hung damp and curling down her back, a couple of stray locks falling into her face. And as she walked toward him, the water moved around her, concealing the most womanly part of her from his view. It changed nothing.

It changed nothing and everything.

It simply was.

And down here, in this ancient, traditional place, ceremonial in many ways, and important to the royal family, it felt sacred.

A confirmation.

One he might have tried to outrun, but he... decided not to.

And so he stood firm and fast as his doom closed the distance between them.

He looked down, saw that her nipples were hard. That her breathing had gone shallow.

"You're right," she said. "I'm not afraid of you." She reached out, delicate fingertips touching the side of his face. They drifted downward slowly, making contact with his broad chest.

Like on the beach. But this time she did not touch him in anger. And this time she didn't stop there. Her hand went down farther. He breathed hard, his stomach pitching as her fingertips ended where the water began. Just above where he was hard and aching for her.

"I didn't understand," she whispered. "But I want to."

"Do you know what you're doing?"

Those green eyes, always filled with challenge, with rebellion, sparked. "Of course I do. I'm not a child. I know what it means to walk into a room with a naked man. To touch him. I know what I'm asking you for."

"But do you know how it will change things?"

For it would. It would change the entire way he had arranged the world.

It would have to.

Damn it all. *Burn* it all.

Tinley Markham was his. Everything else could go straight to hell.

He'd made this choice once before and as he looked at her…he had the sense he would make it again and again until the end of days.

So why not make her a duty, rather than a sin in waiting?

Why not embrace it, and her.

Her body. Her lips. He would sink inside of her

and claim her. And he did not care if his brother had had her first. He didn't care how many men had had her since. She was his and had been from the beginning. Fate.

Destiny.

He alone survived. He alone remained. How could this destiny be denied? How?

It could not be.

He was the Lion of the Dark Wood, and he would devour that which wandered into his path.

He would devour her.

"Yes," she said, her voice thin and breathless.

"And you accept that? All for this? All because your body craves mine?" He studied her closely, the crimson stain in her flushed cheeks. "Do you even like me?"

She shook her head. "No. I don't. But yesterday you made me feel more beautiful than I ever have in my life. I don't *like* you. That's an insipid word. I feel…tormented. My body is not my own. My skin is not mine. It blushes at the memory of you, and becomes sensitive at the thought. Every time my heart beats it's sore. Because it wants to be with the excitement of the touch of your hands. My lips feel swollen, changed. How can I go on if it isn't completed? If this is unfinished?"

There would be no *finish* to this. Not one that either of them would like, not one he was even certain he could live with.

But there was nothing to be done.

There was no turning back.

"You're walking into the wood, little girl? Tell me you understand that."

There was half a breath, a heartbeat, where he thought she might turn away. But then she nodded. "I have to know. I have to know what's on the other side."

It was decided.

He reached out and hooked his arm around her waist, bringing her slick, naked body up against his. Her lush breasts pressed against his chest, and he could swear he almost felt the rapid beat of her heart against his own. He knew that she would be able to feel the hard, insistent length of his arousal pressed against her body.

He was so hard he could scarcely breathe.

He rocked his hips forward, making sure she knew.

And he could tell, by the widening of those eyes, that she felt it.

"I am not an easy man," he ground out. "In this or anything."

"I know."

"You're soft, Tinley. And you have been swaddled and cosseted and protected for all of your life. But I will not do that. No harm will come to you." He slid his thumb over her cheekbone. "But this will not be gentle."

"I don't need gentle." Tears filled her eyes, but he knew they weren't tears of fear. They were defiant. They were angry. "I just need real." She tilted her chin upward. "Tell me that you want me. Tell me that I'm beautiful. Even like this."

"Is that what you need to know? Is it?" He moved his fingers over the freckles on her cheeks, then pushed his fingers through her wet hair. "This. All of this, it tempts me. When you were a girl of eighteen all I wanted was to press you up against the wall and claim you as mine." She was the source of his greatest sin, that girl. And yet she doubted him. But she could never know that. She could never know the truth. "Even when I was angry. Even when I was telling you how unsuitable you were. What I wanted was to sink myself into you and make you mine. You were unsuitable for him. You were supposed to be *mine*."

The words, the ferocity behind them, shocked even himself.

"But not suitable enough to be Queen," she said breathlessly.

"Not suitable for any damn thing. I am a king. And I must keep my head. I am a king, and I must have supreme control over myself and all that I do. And you test that. I am at my end. If you had not been his then…" But it was a lie. He very nearly had. And all that had protected Tinley was his brother's death. "It didn't matter. In the end it didn't matter, did it?"

"You sent me away."

He remembered when she'd come to his office— formerly his father's—after the funeral.

What will I do now?

Anything you wish.

School?

If you desire. There is no more need for you to be here. Of course the palace will care for you, but this is no longer your home.

Guilt and the desire to be rid of her had spurred him on.

"You were happy enough to go."

"I was," she said. "But the speed at which it happened… I had to make a lot of choices and it was overwhelming."

"I was not going to debase myself, or the position of Queen, with my brother's leftovers." Lies on his tongue, bitter. "I was not going to be slave to these feelings."

"And here we are."

So simply she spoke of his failure. So simply she laid out the inevitable.

"I want you," he said. "You must understand, it is not easy."

"I know. It isn't easy for me either."

He didn't have to explain this dark, tortured thing that aided him. Of course he didn't. Because it was like that for her too. There was nothing sweet or simple about it. Nothing misty or magical. This was not fated mates. It was deeper than that. A fated, tortured attraction that existed to make a mockery of all that he was. To make a mockery of whatever power he thought he might possess.

Their desire was the wolf pack. Come to devour them both.

And he surrendered.

He lowered his head and kissed her, harder, darker than yesterday. He plunged his tongue deep into her mouth, wanting to consume her. As she consumed him. Would that it were so simple as want. Would that it were so simple as sex.

Sex was easy. He'd had sex.

This was something else.

This was shame and need and torture all wrapped in a soft, delectable package that he could not turn away from.

He moved his hands to her breasts, cupped them, teased her nipples. For why hold back? Why make slow what had been on the verge of boiling over for all these years?

She gasped, and he took advantage of that. He ate deeper into her mouth, before abandoning her lips and blazing a trail down her vulnerable throat. To her collarbone. He kissed one rounded curve of her breast before taking her nipple deep into his mouth and sucking.

She whimpered, spearing her fingers through his hair and holding him there. As if he would abandon her. As if he would abandon her now that she was finally his.

The only sound in the echoing chamber was their breathing, the gentle sound of the water lapping against their skin. He moved his hands down her body, to her hips, and then, between her thighs where he found her wet and slick and perfect, just waiting for his touch.

His own body pulsed with need. He had never known anything like this. It consumed him.

It was a temptation that surpassed anything he had thought was possible. And the fulfillment of it was beyond anything he had imagined.

Centuries of duty could crumble all around him, he didn't care.

He didn't care.

He moved his hands to her thighs, lifted her up and urged her legs around him, carrying them both up out of the pool.

He walked them both round the bend, to the end of the winding pool. There were low cushions, a cabana of sorts with plush pillows and fabric draped around.

Privacy that was unnecessary, here in this place shared by no one other than royalty.

And as he lowered her down onto the cushions, he asked himself... He asked himself if perhaps he had known that she would be here.

For of course he had given permission for her to use this place to ready herself for the ball.

He had not known when...

But it would stand to reason that she would have been down here. And perhaps he had known.

Perhaps he had always known that in this place, for royalty alone, he would send her to meet her fate.

For if he must be damned by it, then perhaps she should be too.

He stood, looking down at her, her skin pale against the dark red of the cushions. The thatch of curls between her legs aroused him beyond the point of reason.

All of the blood in his body had flowed into the source of his desire, and he felt that he would die for not having her. Which was exactly why he was going to make himself wait longer.

Years.

There were spare few things in this world that he had ever wanted and not been able to have.

He wanted his brothers back, and he could not reach beyond the veil of death to make it so.

And he had wanted Tinley Markham.

Beneath him, astride him, in front of him. However he could have her.

From the moment she had become a woman.

He had wanted her in spite of the fact that she had worn his brother's ring, in spite of the fact that their fathers had decided she would be most suited to marry Dionysus, and not Alex, because God knew the men could've made that determination. It was what Tinley's mother had wanted.

She was correct, in that, the cold hard facts were neither man thought she should be Queen. For had they, she would have been put in the position to be Queen.

And still, he wanted her.

But he was savoring the moment. Savoring the moment where control failed and desire ruled. For this time…this time nothing would stop him. Not when she wanted him as he did her.

Only her.

He knelt down before her, a king on his knees, and brought her body to the edge of the raised cushion, pressing a kiss to her ankle, to her calf, the inner part of her knee. To her side, where she shook beneath his lips.

"Alexius?" She said his name like a prayer, like a question.

Supplication on her lips.

"You know what I intend to do," he said, his voice a growl. "I intend to devour you."

He knew then, that when she had been standing on the edge of the wood, she had been weighing these things. Whether to run into the forest and be devoured by what awaited there, or stay here and be eaten by him.

He was very glad she had chosen the latter.

"I bet you taste sweet," he said. "I have wondered. These long years, I have wondered, what it would be like to feast on you. What it would be like to hear you call out my name, and I intend to. You know how long it has been since anyone has called me Alex? Until you. I would hear that name on your lips as I pleasure you."

He moved higher, his breath on the heart of her now, her sweet scent inflaming him.

Then he lowered his head and slid his tongue over her swollen flesh. Her hips bucked up from the cushion as she whimpered. And he pinned her there, consuming her like a man starving.

For he was.

Starving for her. For all that she was.

He consumed her like he would die if he did not, because he thought he might. Gorged himself on her. On her beauty. On her essence.

He pushed two fingers deep inside of her and found her tighter than anticipated. So he teased her, toyed with her until he began to feel her internal muscles quiver around him. Until he could feel her orgasm building.

Then he sucked that bundle of nerves at the apex of her thighs, and he felt her break. She twisted and writhed beneath him, her release a relief to them both. For he had little control left, and none he could exercise anymore.

He moved up her body and kissed her, deep and long, and then, finally, he thrust inside of her body.

CHAPTER EIGHT

TINLEY WAS STILL trying to recover from the earth-shattering pleasure that Alex had given her, when he breached her.

It *hurt*.

It nearly took her breath away, as powerful as the pleasure that had come before it.

He was so big. When she had seen his body, she had been terrified for a moment, but then he had begun doing all those wicked, pleasurable things to her and it had been difficult to think. No, not difficult, impossible.

And everything he had done to her felt so lovely, his tongue slick and perfect, his fingers knowing and deft, and he had penetrated her that way, and she had thought perhaps it would take some of the difficulty away from their actual joining.

It did not.

Panic rose in her breast.

Courage.

It was a strange thing, to call out for courage for

something she was the one who had initiated. Something she had chosen to do.

But it was frightening. And it was all a bit too much.

And he was…

He was so large and hard and everything. And having him inside of her was beyond anything she could have imagined. For she had known that it might be intense, but she hadn't really known.

It was as if he was inside of her, not just in a physical sense. But in all the ways he could be. As if he inhabited her soul.

It was terrifying. And so was he.

His expression was intense, his big body frozen atop her.

"Tinley?"

"I… I didn't know."

"How?"

Confusion swarmed her. "I… How could I?"

He looked tortured then, his dark brows locked together, his teeth clenched.

"Are you all right?"

"No," she said.

"We'll stop."

"No," she said.

Courage.

"I want this."

Because she had to do this. She had to. He was the lion. The wolf pack.

The dragon.

And she was not a virgin sacrifice. She was a knight, needing to slay him.

Needing to slay this.

So that she could become... Whatever it was she needed to be.

But if she backed away now, then it would still be unfinished. If she backed away now then she would never know.

And she had to know.

She had to.

He pushed deeper inside of her, and she hadn't known it was possible. But finally, some of the pain began to recede, and it gave way to pleasure.

Or, if not pleasure, then something infinitely better than what had come before.

This was different, though, from the easy pleasure she had found from his mouth.

This was something more. It went deep inside of her, and seemed to weave itself in the fabric of her soul.

Created in her a symphony of desire that wrapped itself around her every cell, her every vein, every fiber of what she was.

Until she became part of him.

And he became part of her.

There was a depth to it she could not fathom.

An intensity she could not pin down.

And somehow she knew, this wasn't about sex. This was about the two of them.

About the things that had existed between them for all time.

About fate.

And when he began to move, all the glimmering strands of pleasure that had woven themselves through her began to sparkle. Shimmer.

They warmed her and filled her, changed her. Consumed her. Until she was a creature made entirely of need.

Alex's creature.

But when she saw his face, when she saw the cords in his neck standing out, when she saw the intensity in every line of his big, muscled body, she realized that he was her creature all the same.

That they were one with this, and with each other.

This man who was so different than she.

Who was duty and honor and perfection.

They were the same.

In this, they were equal.

In this, they were remade.

His thrusts were deep, consuming, and she wrapped her legs around him, urging him deeper now, for the pain was gone, and all that remained was wonder.

She didn't think she could possibly be stretched any tighter, didn't think she could possibly scale to higher heights, but she did.

She did.

And each movement of his body within hers did it.

Each rush of his hands over her curves, his lips on her neck, on her mouth.

And then, he lost the rhythm entirely. Splintering into something golden and bright and sweeping her up and all of the fractured edges. And when they broke for the last time, it was together, harsh cries escaping them both at once as he pulsed inside of her and she gripped him tight, wringing every last bit of pleasure from each other as they found their ultimate release.

And then she lay there, knowing that she had been utterly changed.

Knowing that she had lied to herself when she had said she was simply on a quest for courage and closure and an end.

For she had begun something here in this place, and had seen herself utterly changed as a result.

And she did not know how she would find a way back from it.

You won't. You'll have to find a new way.

Everything made sense then.

For that was the truth of it.

She had been trying for all of these years to make sense of an old path that no longer went anywhere.

To go over old wounds, over and over again without actually finding a way to heal them.

To sink into a life that she cared about—undoubtedly—but in such a way that she held herself back for the simple reason of wanting to show her mother she was wrong about her. That she was wrong about her needing to change in any way at all.

There were things she needed to change.

And it might not be about hair or any of the shallow things her mother had fixated on, but there was truth buried beneath the criticism, and being angry about it wouldn't do anything to change that. And rebelling against it for the sake of it wouldn't fix anything either.

He moved away from her, his expression grim.

"Why didn't you tell me?"

"Tell you what?"

"You hadn't had a lover."

"I thought... I didn't think it would be terribly surprising."

"My brother slept with... Anything and everything. The fact that he did not sleep with you is unfathomable to me."

"All you would've had to do was ask. I wasn't ashamed of it. I assumed... I assumed for a long time that he didn't out of respect for my father. Because he was... I don't know. It was some kind of virgin bride thing, I figured. Now I just think maybe we didn't have chemistry." She felt humiliated and small. And it wasn't about the fact that she hadn't had sex with Dionysus. That didn't embarrass her.

It was that she didn't recognize all she hadn't known.

She felt ignorant, and ridiculous, and she hated that most of all.

"It would never have occurred to me he would not have had you the minute it was justifiable."

"Well, he didn't," she said. "You don't have to rub it in."

"Does it bother you greatly?"

"No. I said it didn't. I mean it. I've never been... wounded about that."

He frowned. "You loved him, and you were never sorry that you missed a chance to be his lover?"

"I was young," she said, her face hot. "I didn't know. I don't want to talk about this with you minutes after losing my virginity to you, thank you."

"You should have told me. I would've been more gentle with you."

"All the more reason to not tell you. I didn't need you to be gentle with me. I just needed this to be done."

"Oh, is that all you needed? Was I an itch you needed to scratch?"

She didn't like the sound of that. And she could tell by the disdain in his tone that he did neither. But he wasn't being nice to her, and she found that she perversely wanted to exercise the power that she seemed to have to upset him. Because she felt vulnerable. And she didn't like it.

"I guess so. A question I needed answered. Something owed to me by the royal family, after all. I haven't had a lover. It seemed time that I did. I didn't really want to be trotted out to a roomful of men that I might be married off to not knowing exactly what I was agreeing to. I had never even seen a naked man until you. So, now I know more or less what to expect."

He chuckled. The sound dark. "No. Trust me, *cara*, you don't."

She narrowed her eyes. "Oh. Are you one of those men quite confident in your singularity?"

He lifted his dark brow, and as she was fully able

to gaze upon his singularity in the moment, and as he stood there naked, unabashed and unashamed, she was certain that most men did not match him for size. They couldn't possibly.

He was far too…much to be anything beyond above average.

"Now I know," she said. "I thank you for that."

Her clothes weren't here, so she gathered up her dignity as best she could, and walked away, knowing that he could see all of her bare skin as she tried to keep her head high and walked next to the winding pool, back toward where she had abandoned her clothes. It meant going through that hot water again, and back through the ice.

And by the time she was in her room, she was shivering and miserable, and felt nothing like the luxuriously appointed Royal she was sure she had been meant to feel like by the end of an afternoon spent in that spot.

No. She felt ruined. Unmade, without being remade all the way.

She felt…

Broken.

With a spirit of rebellion, she put her leggings and sweatshirt on, refused to put any product in her hair, knowing it would dry frizzy.

With Algie safely in his carrier, she took Nancy and Alton out of their cage, and placed them on the bed, letting them both trundle around while she tried to find enjoyment in their cuteness. She had been effortlessly charmed by them before.

She was not charmed now.

Peregrine chattered from his cage in clear indignation.

Join the club.

"I can't please everyone," she threw a hand out wide. "You don't get along." She frowned deeply at the ferret and added, "And it's not my fault you're mean."

She would've liked to shout that at Alex.

"It's not my fault you're mean," she repeated again. "And completely unreasonable. And… And… And *why did it have to be you*? Why did it have to be you that I wanted so much? Why couldn't it have been anyone or anything else? And why didn't you warn me that it would…"

Her stomach hollowed out suddenly and she lost all her anger, overtaken completely by abject misery.

She slowly unfolded herself onto the mattress, pressing her face firmly against the bedspread. One of the hedgehogs crawled up onto her back, and over the other side.

It summed up her feeling perfectly.

She had thought she would come out the other side of this feeling empowered, courageous.

Like a woman.

Instead, she rather felt like a hedgehog doormat.

It was not empowering in the least. It wasn't anything except for sad and tomorrow… Tomorrow she was supposed to go into a ball and be presented to all these men. And decide who she was going to marry.

A flame lit itself in her breast. And that was when she knew.

That she had needed to do this. She had. Because she might have balked if she'd not had this experience. She might not have been able to be brave enough.

For tomorrow, when she was introduced, she was going to make the announcement that she was not going to marry anyone. She was going to find a way to make a life on her own terms.

And the one thing she had done for herself...

She had made it impossible to stay here. Impossible to stay connected to Alex.

He was engaged to another woman. However unofficially as far as a love match went.

She would never be able to face his wife. Not after she had seen him naked. Not after he had been inside of her.

And there was no question of her marrying another man. None at all.

She had sealed her own fate, and even though much of what she had done had been foolish she could not regret that. At least, in the story of her life, she had been the author of this particularly inglorious moment.

She would not pawn the credit off to fate.

She would take it all.

And she would take it with pride, even if she couldn't take it with happiness.

And she would have to hope that someday she could.

Even if it would be someday very far away from here.

Even if it would be a someday without Alex.

CHAPTER NINE

HE HAD HANDLED the aftermath of their encounter badly.

But his thoughts had still been swirling with the truth of it all. That Tinley had been a virgin. That she was his, and only his. That she had not been with his brother.

He did not know why he should care, except that he felt no man particularly wanted to have a woman after his brother had had her. For a variety of reasons. And he was no different.

And there was something… Something extraordinary about it. His.

Except, he had wounded her gravely, and now the time of the ball was drawing near and he had not had a chance to speak with her. But perhaps it was better for that. Perhaps, the time for conversation was over. They didn't do well when they conversed with each other, but they did quite well when their bodies met.

Being inside of Tinley was unlike anything he had ever experienced before.

It had been a baptism. A revelation.

It had been…

It had been wrong. But it had also been something to chart a course by. It had made decisions out of problems, and for that, he was grateful. For that, there was nothing to be but grateful.

He was certain that his decision would cause irritation, after all, his PA had certainly made it clear to some of the men that the reason for coming to this event was to look for a prospective wife, one who had the full support of the crown of Liri, but… No one would express their displeasure, for Alexius was the King. And in the end, that was all that mattered.

The King would do what he willed.

And there would be whispers. For there always were.

He was done trying to silence whispers.

He was done denying that which he desired.

He came around the corner, toward the ballroom, just as Tinley came around the curve of the sweeping staircase that led to the antechamber.

His heart stopped in his chest. And then raced forward, as if it was on the verge of exploding.

Her red hair was loose, save for two small strands which had been woven back, and twined together. It was full and curling, and devastating. Her body was wrapped in a gold gown, which made her curves look gilded.

She had barely any makeup on her face, gloss on her lips and something shiny on her cheeks, but her freckles were still clearly visible. She looked like a nymph, a fairy. Something that had come straight from the Dark Wood.

An enchantment.

Or a curse.

She tilted her chin upward, her expression proud. "You look beautiful."

She stopped. "I do?"

"You know you do. You're a triumph."

He took her arm, and he could feel her resist his hold.

"We will go in together."

"All right."

There was a determination about her, that light in her green eyes that he knew well, and he had the feeling that she had a plan of her own.

Whatever it was, it didn't matter to him. For his course was set. And he was the King. And so his course was the course for Liri.

They walked into the ballroom, which was already filled with guests. It was customary for the King to arrive late, as a formal presentation of his royal personage.

But he had a feeling that what Tinley did not understand was that she was being formally presented as well. And not as a mere ward of the crown.

When the double doors opened and they walked into the room, everything stopped. He looked out over the crowd of people. "Good evening. On behalf of the royal family of Liri, I welcome you." It was a customary greeting, but one that was grim these days, considering he was the last remaining Royal.

"Tonight is very special indeed, as I am present-ing to you my future Queen. Ms. Tinley Markham of Liri."

Tinley could hardly believe what she had just heard. The future Queen? There was no way. She had been about to tell him that she was going to marry no one.

That she would be presented to no one. That she would go off on her own and start afresh. And he was engaged to someone else. She turned her head sharply, and met fierce, dark eyes that invited no argument at all.

And she had no idea what she was supposed to do. What she could do. For he was the King, and she could hardly defy him openly in his own ballroom. And soon, they had been swept away from the stair-case that acted as a stage, and he drew her out to the center of the room. To the dance floor. He looked at her, his gaze uncompromising. And it reminded her of that moment in the baths.

They had not seen each other in the hours since, much less touched, and now she was in his arms. And any ferocity or resolution was quashed by the fact that being in his arms stole her ability to think.

Have courage.

That voice echoed inside of her, and she had no idea where it came from, or how it applied now. What courage was there to have? She was in the arms of a king, held prisoner in a room full of hundreds of people, all who glittered. It was a spectacular, gilded show of imprisonment.

And it wasn't fear of reprisal that stopped her. For part of her sensed that it would be easy to speak up now and burn it all down.

To shout that she had no intention whatsoever of becoming the wife of Alexius. That she was not going to be Queen.

Oh, the idea of being *Queen*.

Of being paraded around in front of people at all times.

Influence.

The power to make change.

A queen had that. She also would have the eyes of the world on her.

Yes, it would be easy to run away. It would be easy to defy him, as she did it at every turn. She knew Alex well enough to know that it wasn't exactly like he was going to shift her off to the dark forest and have her executed by a wolf.

No, he wouldn't do that.

The much more terrifying thing was seeing where this might go.

As she had done in the baths.

For she couldn't run then. She could have told him that she didn't want him. That it was a lie. That whatever he thought was happening between the two of them, it wasn't.

That she was naked by circumstance, and not because she had chosen to come down there and seduce him.

And she hadn't.

But she had taken a step toward him because that step put her on the path to a different life.

And this one…

She looked up at him, at this man that seemed as if he were carved from granite.

He was the more dangerous choice. Not defying him. Staying with him.

And when they began to dance, she didn't feel clumsy. She didn't feel awkward. And she didn't know if she was truly skilled all of a sudden or not. It was entirely possible that the sensation she had that she was flying had nothing to do with reality, but only the fact that she was in his arms.

She hadn't the faintest idea why that suddenly made a difference.

Hadn't any idea what it might mean.

That she suddenly felt right, in place, in his arms in spite of the fact that everyone was staring. In spite of the fact that, to an extent this was adjacent to her worst nightmare.

And so they danced, with all eyes on them, but she didn't feel it at all. She felt nothing but the strength of his hold, the warmth of his body.

"Alex," she whispered. "Why didn't you tell me?"

"Why would I?" The question was spoken with such finality, such authority. And there was a faint undertone of…wonder. As if it would never occur to him to consult her on the subject of marrying him.

It was so very Alex.

"To give me some warning."

"And to give you a chance to leave?"

"What if I wanted to leave? Would that matter to you?"

"I am not a man who makes decisions lightly." As if the very fact he'd made a decision was the only thing that truly mattered.

He didn't care what she wanted, only what he thought was best. She thought of the other woman he'd told her he was going to marry.

"What about Nadia?"

He twirled her, and then brought her back close to his body. "She has been informed. Our arrangement was only ever one on paper. It was not a matter of the heart."

She moved her hand from his shoulder, down to his chest. He looked at her, the glint in his eyes sharp. She wondered if she had gone too far. If touching him this way in a room full of people was too...

But the spark in his eyes smoldered, and she leaned into him, into this.

She could feel his heart thundering beneath her palm.

"Ours is a matter of passion, don't you agree?"

Not the heart. *His* heart, which she could feel even now.

"What does that have to do with the royal marriage?"

"There are certain things that are unacceptable to me," he said. "Certain things I will never be able to reconcile. I could never condone infidelity, not in a marriage. Though I considered making the arrangement. Once." That last part was spoken softly, deadly. And the way his dark eyes settled on her made her feel...

"Me?"

"I wanted you when you were his. And I could've taken you. I could have." There was an intensity to his tone that echoed inside her. In her soul.

She knew that it was true. For he was the future King, to Dionysus's future Prince, and Alexius's authority would always be superior. And she...she would have been unable to resist the temptation. She knew that now. For all the simmering fire inside her when she looked at him wasn't hate and it never had been.

In her innocence, she'd thought that discomfort had to be anger. But no. It was desire. Desire for a man she knew she couldn't have. And what would have happened if he'd made it known he wanted her?

The same thing that was happening between them now, and there was no use denying it.

"I was tempted," he said. "But fate...had other ideas. And I'm not the man I was then."

The little bubble of hope that had welled up inside of her fizzled out. It didn't die, because she was much more resilient than that. If she were so fragile that mere words could kill every ounce of hope inside of her she would have lost it, all of it, long ago. At the hands of her mother. Who had been nothing but scathing about her and her accomplishments ever.

Alexius didn't love her. He didn't care for her. If he could have justified sex without marriage he would have done so.

But he couldn't.

So here she was. Not subject to the whims of fate, but to his medieval code of honor.

And as small as it seemed, in this moment, the worst part of all was that her mother would win, her mother would get what she had always wanted. Her daughter as Queen. But under the worst circumstances possible. Her mother, who wasn't even here. Who Tinley hadn't seen in years. Because her father had died, the King had died, Dionysus had died. Every link her mother had to power in Liri was gone, and so she had just… Well, she'd gone off and made another life. A better one.

For Tinley, enough on her own wasn't enough.

And now, by default, she would become the thing that her mother had always wanted.

She wanted to reject it. She wanted to turn away from it. She didn't want to give her mother the satisfaction.

But she also didn't…

She didn't want to live for her mother. Or against her.

She wanted Alex, but she couldn't explain what that meant or why.

It wasn't just sex, but a threat that seemed to bond them together, deeper than she could explain even to herself.

She searched his dark gaze, looking to see if she might find something she recognized there. Something she felt echoing inside of her own chest.

She saw nothing but darkness.

Like standing on the edge of the wood.

"You know, usually a man asks the woman if she wants to marry him," she said softly.

"That implies you have a choice."

"I could leave. You act like I'm more afraid of having nothing than of all this. And that isn't necessarily true."

"And will you leave? You're right. I would not stop you. I would not imprison you. Walk out the door. Tell everyone here that you will not be my Queen."

"No," Tinley said. "I will be your Queen."

Something shivered inside of her. It terrified her. Unto her soul.

"I'm glad we could come to an agreement."

"Good. Think of it as an agreement. Because you should understand that I do have a choice. I had a choice when I went to you yesterday. It was my choice to stay there. It was my choice to take a step toward you, rather than run away. Just as this is my choice now. Don't mistake me, Alex. I'm not afraid of being left with nothing. There are things far worse in the world."

Like trying and failing. Wanting to live up to the standards of another person, only to find that it was impossible. And this put her square in the path of all those fears.

But deeper than her fear she wanted… What she wanted was to explore the dark link she felt with Alex.

It was something new and exciting and magic.

Or perhaps it was old magic.

That truth echoed inside of her.

This thing between them wasn't new at all.

He'd said that he'd nearly claimed her. Taken advantage of his power and taken her back when she'd been with his brother.

And what she had always deemed to be dislike felt like it was something else altogether.

She had been so convinced that she *loved* Dionysus, but here she was agreeing to marry his brother.

His brother who was different from him in every way.

She did not understand herself.

And she needed time to understand herself, and running away wouldn't help.

She'd been running for years now.

They finished the dance, and the rest of the evening went by in a strange blur.

They were on the receiving end of many congratulations, though some of the interactions were with men, and they were quite strange.

"They thought they were coming here to view you as a potential bride," Alex said at one point, as he handed her a glass of champagne.

The glass was crystal, the stem a tree, the branches wrapped around the cup. It reminded her of the wood, encroaching on her.

"And you announced that you were going to instead."

"Yes."

"What must it be like, to wander through life

without fear of reprisal. Most people would never be so bold."

"I am not most people."

"No indeed. Sometimes I wonder if you're a man at all."

His dark gaze burned into her. "Do you? Perhaps I have not made it sufficiently clear."

A thrill raced down her spine. She was frustrated with herself. That she would be consumed with his brand of sexuality while there were much larger things at stake.

But there was only so much that could be spoken about here, in a ballroom full of hundreds of people. There was only so much that could be said.

For she had discovered more about herself and more about him and the time they had spent with no words at all.

Everything that had happened after they'd had sex had been… Wrong. It had driven a wedge between them.

She had felt vulnerable and hurt, and small because of what he had said. And then he had surprised her by declaring that she would be his Queen.

She could not join up the two moments. But she had a feeling that the truth, the answer, was somewhere in that physical connection they shared.

It had to be.

For there was something between them that burned hot and bright, and there was no explaining it. No untangling it with mere words.

They had known each other for years. They had not managed it.

And when the evening wound to a close, she did not know what to expect. For it was late, and there were so many unspoken things between the two of them, they could fill a novel with it.

"I'm hungry," she said.

"You're hungry?"

"I never got a chance to have anything during the ball. People kept talking to me."

"Something we will solve," he said.

He strode toward the dining room, and she lifted her dress up off the floor so she could try to keep up with him. He sat at the head of the table, and she took a seat next to his right.

"Food will arrive soon."

"You didn't…ask for any."

"I am here," he said. "Seated at the dining table. My request is clear. And it will be met."

He wasn't wrong. Moments later, trays of food were brought out before them, savory and sweet, more than she would have ever thought to ask for.

"This is… This is a bit much."

"This is what it is to be royalty."

"Yes. I'm seeing that. I spent a lot of time in the palace but not… There's so much that I don't know. Alex, I've known you for years, but I don't know you." She put her hand on his arm, and his gaze burned with unspoken things. "I want to know you, Alex."

CHAPTER TEN

"A KING IS not meant to be known."

"But I can't live that way. I can't live not knowing you. We are going to be married, and I need to understand you."

He frowned. "There's nothing to understand. I'm a king. You will be my Queen."

"Those are both labels, not personalities." She looked at him. Hard. "I'm Tinley. You think that I'm too loud, and a bit clumsy. I like to knit. I enjoy baking. I hope I'll be allowed to do some of that even after we've married. I like animals. The charity that I'm affiliated with is very important to me." Her heart squeezed. "Because I know what it's like to have my mother look at me and think that there's something wrong with me. And the children my charity benefits live in a world that isn't made for them. And in every way, big and small every day, they are made to feel like they're wrong. Because they have neurological differences. Because they have different ways of thinking and learning. Because nothing in the world, in their school, is made for them. And

I'm passionate about creating ways for them to be able to feel like they belong. Because all I have ever wanted is to feel like I belonged. It isn't the same. I don't have the same challenges they do. But I understand the feeling. And if I can help spare even one person a measure of that, then I will. I hope in my position as Queen I can further that."

"Undoubtedly," he said, visibly unaffected by her speech. "As Queen of Liri you will have money and influence at your disposal. Invest in whatever you like. You will be able to raise the profile for your convictions with ease."

"Well. Good."

She studied him, trying to see if what she had said had… Meant anything to him. Sunken at all. Because it felt important that he understand. She was… She was so tired of being alone.

A feeling…

Nobody knew her. Not really.

She'd made decent friends when she'd gone away to school, but none of them could really understand what her life had been like. Many of them were from privileged backgrounds, it was true, but none of them had been engaged to a prince.

She had experienced a measure of pretty intense grief at only eighteen.

She had lost the future she'd been dreaming of. She had rebuilt herself to an extent. But the more she thought about it the more she realized that in every space she'd ever occupied, from being Dionysus's fiancée, to being a college student, to working at a charity, to being here now, she had only ever given pieces of herself in those places.

No one had all of her.

Sometimes she wasn't even entirely certain she had all of her.

"Were you not hungry?"

She nodded, and reached out and took a stuffed date from one of the trays. It was good, but her hunger was no longer the most pressing issue she faced. It was this strange, desperate feeling of isolation, and the desire to be rid of it.

"What do you care about?" she asked.

"Being the King my country needs."

It was like flinging herself at a brick wall. "But what do *you* care about. You're not just a king, Alex. You're a man. And I can't… Nothing in this castle is yours. It's all your father's. All your ancestors'. Even the scolding you gave me that night at the state dinner back when I was engaged to Dionysus… That wasn't yours either. It was what you thought you had to do to behave in a way that fit the crown. But what do you care about?"

"You're wrong about one thing, Tinley, King is not just a title. It must be who I am. All of who I am. It is essential. For it is in the man that you find weakness. I can afford no more weakness."

"If you mean Dionysus… It's ridiculous that anyone blames you. And I'm sorry that I've been one of them. I felt… I cared about your brother very much. And for a whole lot of my life I was convinced that I loved him. He was easy to love. I got angry at you yesterday because I had to face how foolish I was to not realize that he didn't love me back. The things that I excused, and the things that I decided had explanations… They were born of naivety. Nobody wants to believe that they are naïve. But I was. I am. I felt like a silly child next to you yesterday, and I hated it. Because we were naked together. I didn't want to feel that gulf."

She took a deep breath. "You're not responsible for what he did."

"When Lazarus disappeared, it's because I… I forgot myself. I was more interested in fun than doing my duty. We were playing together in the yard. He said he saw something in the forest. Something that moved. And he wanted to see. I… I was tired of him. He was badgering me. I got angry. We were supposed to be playing ball, and it had gone the opposite direction of the wood, and we couldn't find it. I told him to go on then, and he would have to deal with Father. I left him. I went to the hedge to search for the ball. When I turned back, he was gone. Because I was selfish. Because I didn't want to deal with him. Because I didn't want to do my duty. It doesn't matter how old I was. I had a responsibility."

"Alex, you know that's just kid stuff, it's not anything you can be held responsible for."

"Dionysus. I knew he was drunk. You had left the ballroom by that point, so you won't remember this. He was making grand claims about how he was going to brave the wood. About how it was clear he was the real lion. The true heir. He had a woman with him, and he was bound and determined to show off for her. And I… I didn't stop him." There was something strange in his voice. As if he was holding something back, but she couldn't figure out what it might be.

"His decision is not your responsibility."

"I am the King. I am the King and in those moments of weakness, when I was simply a brother, simply a man, I allowed petty things to get in the way of what I knew to be better. What I knew to be true. I did it twice, and the consequences were fatal. No, a man should not blame himself for the actions of others, but a king has no choice. For I hold the future of the nation in my hand. For the responsibility of the people is mine. My brothers were my people. And I did not serve them. I did not protect them. I failed. I made a decision then. To be King. Not Alexius and a king. But King Alexius of Liri. There is no other identity. There is no other piece of me. There cannot be."

"I don't believe that."

"Believe it. It is a decision I made with great weight."

"I can't be just a queen. I can't. I can't disappear behind a façade."

"I would not ask it of you."

"I feel like it puts you on one side of the glass and me on the other."

"I never expected to know my wife."

"And is your… Is your temptation toward me something of the man or the King?"

His posture stiffened, his face turning to stone.

"You're to be my Queen. You are not a temptation."

It was like a brick wall had gone up between them.

Like he was intent on proving something to her. On distancing her.

But she had agreed to marry him. He could not do that. And she couldn't live this way. So near to him, and yet so far.

"Then tell me something else," she said. "If you will not talk of temptation."

Her heart beat a sickening rhythm at the base of her throat. Her hands were damp. Shameful excitement bloomed in her midsection.

And she cast her mind back, to all the times she had catalogued with him over the years. And there was a catalog of encounters, to be sure. She remembered each and every one of them, as if they happened only recently.

"Dionysus made me feel warm. Happy. Accepted. And I understand now that…he had a different plan for our relationship than I did. I understand that what I thought was love between the two of us was… It was not love for him. It wasn't even love for me. I confused friendship for love. And I didn't consider desire at all." She swallowed hard. "That day that you scolded me in the corridor. I felt very upset. My heart beat fast, and my stomach twisted. I thought I was angry. I thought I was furious with you. I wanted to get closer to you. I wanted to hit you. Something.

Make contact. Did I want you? Is that what was happening?"

His face seemed to turn to stone, and a muscle in his jaw jumped, the only sign of life. "I cannot answer that question."

"Your cold fury, your disapproval… I thought about it all the time. Your eyes. The way that you looked at me. It upset me so much, Alex, that I could not make you like me. Dionysus was so easy…"

"There is no benefit to this discussion."

"Was it always going to happen? We'd have found ourselves alone after some party, me the Princess, married to your brother, and… Would we have touched? What about if I had been with him, and what transpired between us didn't make me feel half so much as what looking into your eyes did?"

"Tinley, it doesn't matter. He's dead." Those words came out raw. "You were never with him. And you will be with me."

"I think it matters. Because I want to understand. I want to understand desire. And why it doesn't seem to make sense. Why sometimes it makes it seem like the world is turned inside out. Is it why I make you so furious? Is that why you had to marry me? Because you are afraid if I was wandering around out there married to another man, and you married to another woman that we might… That we might violate who we want to be in order to be with each other?"

"I turned temptation into duty. All in all, I feel it was the best decision I could've made."

"So you were afraid of that. You were afraid of

me. Were you always? Is that why you opposed me so very much when I was engaged to Dionysus?"

"None of this matters."

"It matters to me."

"I told you. I made the decision to be a king, and not a man."

"You outran temptation rather than being potentially subject to it. You would bind yourself to me forever so that you don't ever have to feel weak again."

"If it is a weakness that you're looking for, Tinley, then look no further than this moment here. Does that make you happy? You are correct. What you're reaching around for, searching for… It's true. I made the decision to marry you so that I would not be fallible. Now your body is my duty. Your children will be mine. And there will be no vows to violate."

Her heart pounded in her ears.

"Why does it make you so angry?"

Because that was one thing she couldn't understand. Hadn't he won in some respects, gaining her as a wife? If the temptation of her had vexed him all this time.

"Because nothing should test me in this way."

"Why is that? Does it bother you so much because of the temptation in general? Or because… Because it's me. Because I'm so unsuitable."

He closed the distance between them, cupping her chin, forcing her to look into his eyes. "It is that the strength of my desire for you makes me unsuitable."

And this was it. A window into the man. The man that she was going to marry, for whatever he said, it was not simply the King she would bond herself to for her entire life. For it was not a king looking at her now. He needed to believe it, and she understood that. She understood that the blame that he carried around was heavy on his shoulders. That he believed he couldn't want things for himself. That he couldn't want fun. That he couldn't want pleasure. And he had moved her into the category of duty to sidestep that, and he recognized it was a side step. He had also tried to make it as a grave decision. One that seemed a better choice than simply pining and taking chances.

She wanted to believe it meant there was more, and she couldn't even quite say why, for she was only just beginning to wrap her mind around the fact that she had wanted Alex for quite some time. That Alex was something uniquely special to her. It occurred to her then that maybe there was a difference between the disapproval that her mother had shown her, and the actual feeling Alex had given her when she was near him. Perhaps it wasn't disapproval at all. Perhaps the real issue was that Alex made her feel like she needed to be different, and the idea of having to try like that terrified her. Yes, it was rooted in what her mother had made her feel, because she had gone into her awkward phase, her teenage years, already feeling at a deficit. Already feeling like there was no possible way for her to triumph over the awkwardness she had been born into.

But there was a difference between that, that shallow disapproval of her mother, and limiting herself because she was afraid to be disapproved of. Because she was afraid of trying her absolute hardest and failing.

What an easy thing it was to fail at having straight hair when your hair was frizzy and curly. What a difficult thing it was to try your absolute hardest to be the best, to try to be the Queen and not manage it. It was such a vastly different thing than failing at living up to a standard her mother had invented for her that she didn't even want. One showed her a glimmer of the feeling.

Of feeling like a failure. Of feeling not quite good enough.

The other would be… It would be devastating. To well and truly be rejected by someone she really wanted. Doing something she really wanted to do. Something that mattered.

She had hidden herself away because it was easier.

And this desire to know him… It was deep and real, and it meant she couldn't hide. Not anymore.

So, she clung to that thing he'd said. To that one honest thing. To the fire burning in his eyes.

That to him, the way he wanted her made him unacceptable.

For that was real, and it was human. It was the man and not the King.

And it was what she was desperate for.

It was, she was certain, the place that she would find the answers to what she desperately needed to know.

And so she stood from her chair, and positioned herself in front of him.

"Is it how you want me now?"

"You're to be my Queen."

"Then I'm yours. And you can take me if you want. You can do whatever you like. Because I belong to you."

"Say that again," he said, his voice like iron.

"I belong to you."

He growled, wrapping his arm around her waist and drawing her down onto his lap, she could feel the hardness of his arousal pressing up against her behind.

"You're mine," he said, kissing her jawline. "Mine at last. I've wanted you… It has been like a sickness. But now you belong to me. And no one else. Do you have any idea how intoxicating it was to discover that no other man had ever touched you? Not just my brother, but none of the men at your University? No one. As if you were waiting for me."

She turned to him, conviction burning in her breast. "But I imagine I don't have the same sort of gift. I imagine there have been women. You weren't simply waiting around for me. So, are you to be mine? As I'm yours?"

His eyes went flat. "I belong to Liri. My first service must be to my country."

"So I'm to share you with a nation? While I belong solely to you? That doesn't seem fair."

"Everything here is mine. You among them. It is as fair as anything."

"You belong to me," she said, pressing her forehead to his.

She could never have imagined doing this even weeks ago. Touching Alex like he was a human. Pressing her face to his. So close that she could see the lines at the corners of his eyes, the deep grooves that bracketed his mouth. That she could see the beginnings of his evening beard, dark and heavy on his jaw.

She knew how it felt to be kissed by those firm lips. What it was to feel those whiskers on his face scratching at her skin.

She had been afraid of him. Or rather…wary, because somewhere inside of her she had always known it could be this way. Yes. She had been wary. Desperately so.

And now, it was as if a wall had come down. And she could see him, truly. Challenge him. Touch him.

"You're mine," she whispered. "And I don't care if you believe it. I don't care if you'll admit it. You belong to me, Alex. Me. I had your body inside mine, and I don't care if there have been other women. They weren't me. I'm the one that tempted you. And you don't succumb to temptation."

"Must you believe that?"

"I know it," she said, her voice barely above a whisper.

"I know it." She repeated that again.

He growled, cupped the back of her head and brought her in for a kiss, hard and ferocious. He might not admit to being hers, but she could feel it. Every move of his lips over hers, and the slide of his tongue against hers. The way his hands moved over her body. He was trying to claim possession, but he had already done so. It was that she could feel her own possession in the way they touched. In the way he tasted her. For there was a care in the way he handled her that spoke of someone taking great pains to be gentle with something that was precious to them. Precious belonging.

But there was something deeper and richer underlying it, and she knew. Knew that it was flowing both ways. Knew it to be true.

And if he wouldn't admit, it was all right. She would simply know it in her heart until he could.

And she would try. With everything. Not in the way that she had been.

Not sliding under the radar, hiding out in a cottage in the woods.

No. With everything.

She reached behind her back and undid the zipper on her dress, let it fall to her waist.

The undergarment was built into the gown, and unzipping it left her breasts bare.

"These are yours too," she said, a small smile tugging at her lips. "My body is yours."

It was sort of cheesy, and she felt half silly saying it, but his response wasn't silly at all. He gathered her up in his arms and kissed her. With everything.

It was a claiming. An absolute devastation.

And she loved it.

"Do you have any idea how beautiful you look tonight? Coming down the stairs with your hair loose? It's everything I was afraid to see in you.

Your wildness. Your beauty. Because I was afraid that if I thought, I would not be able to resist it. Disapproval was so much easier."

"And running away was always easier. Pretending that what I felt was fear."

It was true. It was so much easier than this. Than diving headlong into a flame that might consume them both, reduce her to ash, leave her less than nothing.

He was the King, and in the end he would stand, even if he was reduced. But she… She would not. She knew it. With everything inside of her she knew it.

He shifted her on his lap so that she was astride him, so that the very heart of her was pressed against the hardness in the front of his slacks. Then he reached between her thighs and began to stroke her there. He pushed his fingertips beneath the edge of her lace panties, teasing her, finding her wet and ready for him.

She had been ready for him. For so much longer than she'd realized. And she felt no shame at all, golden and brazen in the great dining hall of this palace.

"You were so scathing of my being loud at this table some years ago," she said, wickedness overtaking her. "What do you suppose you would have thought of such a display?"

"I wanted it then," he growled. "Make no mistake. I wanted it then."

Pleasure bloomed low in her stomach and he continued to stroke her, gliding through her pleasure, using his fingers inside of her and tormenting them both. She tilted her hips against his hand, moving with the rhythm of his strokes. Then she reached out and curved her fingers around him through the fabric of his pants, squeezing him before unbuttoning the pants, drawing his zipper down and freeing his hardened masculinity.

He was glorious. The feel of him in her palm satiny and hard. Hot.

"I did not know a man could be so beautiful."

"How can you speak of male beauty when you are here? When you are golden? When you are every fantasy a man could ever possess. Tinley," he said, her name a growl on his lips.

And she burst into flame.

Her climax overtook her, suddenly, radically.

She hadn't been expecting it. Her name on his lips. Her. He wanted her.

King Alex de Prospero wanted her. She was not a second prize, nor was she simply his responsibility, his ward. He wanted her. It was laced into every word he spoke, but most especially into her name.

For she wasn't only a generic woman to him. She had cost something.

And perhaps she wouldn't be able to lay sole claim to his body as he could to hers, but she had that. And it mattered.

He gripped her rear end, pulling her hard against him, his flesh pressed against her aching cleft. He rocked against her, eyes blazing. And she gasped. A pulse beat between her legs, and she felt hollow, desperate for his invasion. But he only teased her, his masculinity growing slick with her desire as he teased them both.

She was gasping, weeping, barely able to breathe as he continued to rock in a maddeningly slow rhythm against her.

With one hand, he gripped the back of her hair, forcing her to keep her gaze steady on his. Then he leaned forward, kissing her, the edge of his teeth scraping her chin, her neck, making his way down to her breasts.

And she felt beautiful. Perfect. Cherished. As he held her like this she felt like everything.

And for a girl who had constantly felt small, diminished, like nothing, it was the most erotic and incredible experience to be had.

He lifted her then, as he stood up, and deposited her on the table. Then he repositioned himself, sliding slowly inside of her. And when he was buried deep, he kissed her. Hard.

She cried out, bucking against him, the pleasure that was pouring through her almost too much to bear. He barely moved, and he sent her straight over the edge again. The climax shocked her, so hard on the heels of the other, and it left her gasping, begging for more. He cupped her breasts, riding her hard, the sound of their mutual need filling the room. He was fully clothed, and she resented it. She wanted him. All of him. Wanted to touch his body. Wanted to claim him, consume him as he was doing her. She ripped his shirt open, wrenched his tie free of his neck. She couldn't stop touching him. Moving her hands all over that golden skin. Every masculine inch of him, as the thickest, hardest part of him filled her to the brim.

"Alex," she called out his name.

"Yes," he growled. "You know who this is. Inside of you. Claiming you."

"Alexius," she said.

The sound of his pleasure became a fury, driving them both to the brink.

"No," she whimpered as she felt another climax rising inside of her. There was no way she could survive it. "I can't. Not again."

"You will," he said.

He reached between their bodies, and closed his thumb and forefinger over her slick lips, pinching the source of her pleasure, and she cried out. "Alex!"

She shattered completely. She couldn't stop. It seemed to go on and on. Over and over again, when surely she must have reached the end of pleasure. The end of being.

The end of the world.

But there at the end, was Alex. His strong arms, his stern face. And it wasn't disapproval that she saw there. It was passion.

It was what always had been there. But it had been banked before, controlled. And now it was rampant. Free. Rioting through them both.

Taking them both to a place she hadn't even realized existed.

Alex.

Of course she had feared him. She had been right to.

For this was blessing and curse rolled into one. This was more than anything had ever been.

Than anything ever could be.

And when he shattered, it sent her over the edge again. Left her a sobbing, gasping mess in his arms.

"My King," she said, putting her fingertips against his lips.

And he shuddered again.

Her King. Hers.

He might have mistaken her, might have thought she was simply using it as a title. But it wasn't. It was more.

Hers.

Her King. Her man.

And hovering around the edges was the truth that she didn't think she wanted.

The truth of her feelings. Of how she really felt.

She hadn't known love. Not before this.

Love.

It made her want to weep. And in her reduced state she didn't think she could handle it.

"Take me to bed," she said.

"As you wish." He righted her down, began to put his own clothes back together as best as he possibly could.

And he lifted her up in his arms. She reached down and grabbed a tray of cheese and meat, holding it in her arms as he held her.

"It seems a shame to waste it," she said as he carried her from the room.

"I doubt I will be hungry for it tonight. Not when I have so much of you to feast on."

Her face went hot. "Well. If it's all the same to you, I might want some protein later."

"Whatever you need to keep up your strength."

He carried her into his bedchamber. She hadn't been here before.

It was expansive and incredible, and the bed at the middle of the room was massive.

"You bring a lot of women here. Because it looks conducive to athletic…"

"No," he said. "This is my space."

"Good," she said. "I find that I'm possessive." He carried her partway into the room. "Go by the dresser."

He looked at her like she was strange, but he complied, and she deposited the tray on the top of it.

"Let it never be said you don't think of the practicalities," he said dryly.

"Well," she said. "I run a charity."

"Indeed," he said.

That stern face. She would give anything to make him laugh, but she knew that he would resist it. With everything he had.

She wanted him to like her cat. To at least tolerate the hedgehogs and the ferret. Because caring for them was part of her. And she wanted to share herself, share her life with him.

But she didn't know if they would ever be able to bridge that.

As he carried her to the bed and set her down at

the center of the large mattress, she found herself releasing that.

It may never happen.

They may never be able to find ground that common.

But they certainly seemed able to find common mattress. And dining table.

Perhaps that would be enough.

Because the naked connection she felt with him here was incredible. Was absolutely everything she could have ever asked for and more.

"My Queen," he said, before he entered her again.

And it wasn't the Queen part that mattered to her.

It was that she was his.

CHAPTER ELEVEN

"WE HAVE CREATED quite a stir," Alexius said, walking into Tinley's bedroom the next day.

She was tucked up on the bed in sweats, her hair a tumble around her. And there was a ferret on the mattress beside her.

"What is the meaning of this?" He gestured toward the animal.

"He's having his exercise."

"Why is there a *rodent* on the mattress?"

"Ferrets are not rodents," she said, her indignance nearly humorous.

"Ferrets *look* like rodents."

"They don't. You can actually tell because of the teeth…"

"Ferrets look like rodents," he said. "In Liri, they are now classified as rodents."

"You can't do that. You can't…" She picked the white drapey animal up from the bedspread. "You can't reclassify an animal just because you want to."

"I think you'll find that I can." Now her fury was amusing.

"Well, it's stupid," she huffed. "And no one will agree with you."

"I think you'll find everyone will agree with me."

She sighed, exasperated, and draped the creature over her shoulder. "What is it you wanted to tell me?"

"We have created quite the stir," he said. "With our engagement."

"Well, that's understandable. Given I was previously engaged to your brother."

"Indeed. Though, the stir that I've created with your mother might be bigger than the stir created worldwide."

"That doesn't surprise me one bit. My mother is deeply avaricious. And I imagine she's thrilled."

"Yes. She misses you."

Tinley frowned. "She doesn't. She's only very happy that she's finally managed to get what she always wanted."

"And that is?"

"The potential position with me as Queen. You should hold him."

"I'm sorry, what?"

"Peregrine. You should get to know Peregrine." She offered up her pet, like a ropey, furry python.

"I will have to decline."

"He means a lot to me."

"How interesting for you."

"You know," she said, "when I came back from school I was feeling really low. And I found out about these animals, which were taken from an animal hoarding room situation. And being able to take care of them made me feel like I was doing something."

He was not interested in the getting-to-know-you thing Tinley seemed bound and determined to enforce between the two of them. But he found…he was interested in her. And that was something he had not anticipated. "You have a real obsession with feeling like you're doing something good."

"Why not? I get tired of feeling like I'm just another pawn. Like I don't really matter. It feels good to be able to actually make an impact. To do something good, rather than just worrying about myself. I've been through a lot of things that were really sad." Something in his heart went tight.

"Not to say you haven't," she said. "But, you have a whole country to do the right thing for. I've had *them*." She indicated her animals.

"And your charity."

"Yes. It's not because I'm very good. Or because I'm uniquely predisposed to being an altruist. It's just that… When things are sad it's very easy to sink into a space where you get tired of yourself. Tired of your own pain. Helping somebody else can take your eyes off of that for a while. It can make things feel better. I was deeply hungry for that when I returned to Liri."

"I can understand that," he said.

"Good."

She had so much passion in everything she did. It shamed him, in some ways. Because he didn't allow himself such measures of feeling. Such an indulgence.

Feelings… Feelings for him had only ever been a bad thing. When those desires began to outweigh his duty, it became a problem. A problem he couldn't afford.

And she had always been a problem.

He had her now, and as long as he kept everything in its rightful place, it would be as it should.

"You can hold him."

"I don't want to."

"For me?"

She smiled at him. And the strangest thing happened. He found himself smiling back. "I'll pet it," he said.

He reached out and brushed his hand over the animal's ears. Tinley lit up like a beacon.

"Is that a smile?" she asked.

"At you," he said, putting his hand back at his side. "And you didn't even get your way. I didn't hold it, I petted it."

"I knew you'd never hold him," she said. "I suggested that so you'd downgrade it to petting. I won."

"You look ridiculously pleased with yourself."

"I am. I only wish I had taken a picture."

"I would have you thrown in the dungeon."

"You're really not so scary."

"I am. I promise you. Ask my enemies."

"You haven't got any, have you?"

"None living. So actually, I suppose you can't ask them. Dead men tell no tales and all of that."

She rolled her eyes at him. "You try to make me believe you're that scary. But I know you're not."

"Do you?"

With an impish grin she reached out and pressed her palm to the front of his pants. "No."

He took hold of her wrist and moved her away from him. "Do not touch me while there are animals present."

She laughed, the sound infectious, and he found himself nearly joining her.

"So what will we do about my mother?" She put the animal back in his cage.

"I suppose we invite her to the wedding. She will know better than to make any comments that will upset you."

"I'm not sure about that."

"Does it bother you?"

"It doesn't bother me, really. That's another thing I realized recently. I spent a lot of time doing things to defy my mother. She had a low opinion of me, and there was a point where for the sake of rebellion, I decided that I wasn't going to try. Not to live up to her expectations. Not at all. And I think I became less than I could be trying to be the opposite of her, rather than just being myself."

"If you don't want her at the wedding," he said, "you only have to say."

"She can come."

Satisfaction burned inside of him. That suddenly Tinley had the power in the situation with her mother. That she was no longer a small child to be made to feel inferior.

It made him… Happy to give her something.

Whether it was holding her pet or giving her the chance to have a victory against the woman who had made her feel less.

Feelings. They had no place in this. Not anything that went deeper than a smile. Longer than a moment.

He pushed them aside. He pushed everything aside. "We will marry as soon as possible."

As soon as possible still meant that it would take some time. But Tinley was okay with that. The sooner the wedding took place the sooner she would have to deal with her mother, and she wasn't looking forward to that. The sooner the wedding took place, the sooner they would have to deal with the public aspect of what they were doing. And she was just enjoying Alex.

He was adamant, of course, that there was nothing more to know about him. But being with him taught her things that words he spoke never could.

She slept in his bed at night and fell asleep in his strong arms. He saw her in the morning when she woke up, an absolute mess, but smiling. And he seemed to want her all the same. It didn't matter if she was dressed for dinner or in her pajamas that had little badgers all over them. Though, he'd made it clear he preferred her out of them, and typically stripped her naked the minute she appeared wearing the cozy garments.

She didn't mind.

Because she liked being naked with him. Because when she was naked with him, she learned things not just about him, but about herself.

She had always thought that she would end up with someone funny.

Dionysus had been like that. Funny and light and easy to get along with.

Alex was… He was dark.

But there was a gravity to his seriousness that made her feel anchored to the earth.

A loyalty in him that she had never witnessed in anyone else.

It made a deep quiet move in her soul.

A security that surpassed all she had ever known.

For when Alex said he would be true to her, she had no doubt he meant it.

She had no real doubt that Dionysus would have meant it either, it was just that she would've doubted his ability to keep his promise.

Alex's promises were part of who he was.

He was a rock, a mountain, a predator. All those things that she thought of him as before.

But she had missed a few crucial things about that characterization.

A mountain was strong, and it would not easily crumble.

Wolves, lions…they protected their pride. Led

their packs. They were not solitary, and they did not turn and eat their own.

No. They were the leaders. The protectors.

That was Alex.

And he had brought her in and made her part of him, and that meant that he would die for her.

Kill for her.

She had been loved before.

Her father really had loved her, and she didn't doubt it.

But the arrangement he'd made with her and Dionysus had been about him. He hadn't thought it would make her miserable, of course. But Alex had said... her father was human.

This command that she marry Alex, though, it was about managing his own temptation...

It was about her. About who she was in the fact that he could not turn away from her.

And she wouldn't say that Alex loved her.

But she had become his.

And in his world she felt it was the same thing. If not more. If not deeper.

And tonight she had enticed him out to the garden. It was warm, and beautiful outside, the twilight settling down over them like a veil, the light strong overhead in the garden illuminating them.

She was letting Algernon pounce off some of his fatness, though mostly, the cat was interested only in rolling in the grass, and not actually getting any exercise.

Alex, being Alex, was standing there in his dark suit and shoes, his expression like stone.

Tinley was barefoot, wearing a dress, her hair loose. Her cat was currently on his back, wiggling around in the soft blades of grass, and Tinley giggled, lying down on the grass beside him and rolling onto her own back.

"What is it you're doing?"

"Enjoying myself," she said. "You know, you might benefit from enjoying yourself."

"I'm opposed."

She shifted, letting her dress ride up around her thighs. There was no one out here. No one but them. Well, and the cat. He did have a strict rule about the fact that she wasn't permitted to try anything when there were animals watching.

It was fair enough, she had to admit. It was a little bit disconcerting. But sometimes she forgot, and lost herself in looking at his stern male beauty, and the fact that there was a cat around was the furthest thing from her mind.

Anyway, the cat couldn't talk. It's not like he was going to tell tales.

His gaze sharpened, looking at her bare legs.

"You can come down here and join me."

"I don't…sit in the grass."

"You don't think you'd ever make love in the grass?"

The corner of his mouth turned upward, and she found herself pinned to the earth, his great, muscular form come down on top of her at the speed of light. "That is a different suggestion altogether."

The show of humor, playfulness, coming from Alex buoyed her. She lifted her head up from the ground and bit his lip. He growled, gripping her wrists and drawing them up over her head, flexing his hips forward and letting her feel his hardness.

"Very wicked," she said. "Much more wicked than I ever thought I could be."

"I always knew I could be," he said, his voice suddenly rough. "At least, I always knew I could be with you."

He said things like that, and it made her feel special. Made her feel like this was so singular and special nothing else could ever come close to it. Ever.

Which made her special, and that, above all else was a revelation. He was a mountain, it was true, and everything good that went with it. But he would also get down on the ground for her, with her. She made him smile.

She touched the stern lines around his mouth.

"What?"

"Nothing," she said. "Except you know I find you impossibly beautiful."

"Beautiful," he said, his voice filled with disdain.

"Yes, beautiful. Such a beautiful man."

"Tinley," he said, his voice rough. "I would have you…"

"People could come out," she said, feeling slightly nervous about being too much of an exhibitionist. The baths were one thing. The garden was another.

"Too much staff and all of that. Oh, could we…? Could we have a picnic?"

"A picnic?"

"Yes. Come on. It will be fun."

"Fun? Eating out here on the ground?"

"Yes," she said. "I'll even put Algie back in his cage, and take him inside. And then it will just be you and I out here. And whatever happened after the picnic…"

"It would make you happy?"

"Yes," she said.

Something shifted in his expression. "It is so simple to please you?"

She reached out and touched his hand. "It can be."

She could see, for just a moment, emotion in his dark eyes. "I will arrange it."

He stood, and made his way quickly back to the castle, and Tinley laughed at his retreating figure. He wanted her. It was a wonderful revelation. Just then, something caught Algernon's attention, and he sat up, his ears facing forward. The little cat was never that alert, and Tinley thought it was odd. He was staring into the woods.

"All right," she said, "let's get you back—"

The cat sprang into action, and then ran into the forest, disappearing from view before Tinley could grab him.

She stood, staring after him. He couldn't have gone far. He was only capable of short bursts of speed. She sighed heavily and took a step toward the forest. Dread crept over her. She knew that she wasn't supposed to do this. Knew that she wasn't supposed to go here.

Alex would be furious.

"And I'll be back before he is."

And on a deep breath, Tinley slipped into the trees.

CHAPTER TWELVE

WHEN ALEX RETURNED from the palace, he found the garden empty.

Tinley wasn't there. Her cat wasn't even there.

A wash of dread went over him.

And he knew. He knew exactly where she was and what had happened.

He had let his guard down.

And it happened again.

Fury rose up inside of him, and he charged headlong into the forest without thinking.

It was dark here under the trees. Completely black.

It was evening as it was, and here beneath the canopy of trees, there was nothing. Panic ate at him.

For he knew exactly what could happen here. And so did she. She knew better than this. She knew better than to play around with this.

Perhaps this is it. The end of the curse.

Everyone who touches you dies.

He gritted his teeth. There was no point in thinking that way. Not with Tinley lost in the woods, and with nothing to be done for her except find her.

He pushed through the trees, listening intently for anything he might hear.

He heard the howl of a wolf, and the hair on his arms rose on end.

He took two steps forward, found a large tree branch and held it like a club. An entire pack of wolves would be no match for his fury. Anything that dared touch Tinley was already dead. Man or beast.

There were no paths in the wood, and the trees reached out to grab him, and he elbowed his way through. Listening. He didn't want to call out, for some reason. Something inside of him prevented it. And he felt the need to trust that sensation.

For he always did.

The kingdom of Liri was an ancient one, and the only thing more feared than the wood itself was superstition of what might happen if it was destroyed. That sense of old-world magic was something he still carried inside himself, though he was pragmatic in many ways.

He felt the weight of the mystical here.

And if nothing half so fanciful as old magic lived here, then many animals did. Trees. A delicate ecosystem that scarcely existed anywhere in the world before. It was for men to be respectful of it. Careful of it. Not to destroy that which they could not dominate.

Even he believed that.

He heard another wolf howl, and that was when he

knew the silence had to end. He growled in response, and pressed forward quickly, bursting through the trees and into a clearing. Tinley was sitting there, clutching her cat, looking wide-eyed.

"Get up," he commanded, reaching his hand out.

She looked up at him, a mixture of gratitude and fear in her eyes. "Come with me," he said.

She didn't need to be asked twice.

He hauled her up off of the ground and brought her up against his chest. "What were you thinking?"

"Can we get out of the terrifying forest, please?"

"Nothing will touch us." He looked around. "You're with me."

He propelled them both back through the woods, back toward the palace, and when they were on the grounds again, free of the oppressive darkness of the trees, he rounded on her. "What the hell were you thinking?"

"Algie… He went into the trees. I was sure that he was only just a little bit away, but then he was gone. I found him and that clearing, and I have no idea how he covered so much ground so quickly. But I was about to walk back out, when I heard the wolves. And I needed to figure out which direction they were coming from…"

"Every direction," he said, his voice hard. "You can never let your guard down like that again. Ever. You cannot expose yourself to such dangers, Tinley. I forbid it."

"I know. But it's… It's only a forest, and nothing is cursed. I understand that people have died going into it, but many people have gone into it and not died."

"It's only the people who have were my brothers."

"I know," she said. "I'm sorry."

"It will not happen again," he said, his voice stern.

"No, it won't. I... I'm sorry. But everything's okay." She looked around and saw the picnic that he had brought out for them. "Let's have dinner."

"No. There will be no picnic."

"Why not?"

"You're not to go in the garden anymore. Not for a while."

"Are you... You putting me under house arrest?"

"If I must. I will. It concerns me not in the least to cut you off of the outside world if I have to do it to keep you safe."

"Alex..."

She could have been killed. The idea of coming upon her...her blood staining the ground. For the first time he was tempted to tear the forest apart. Raze it to the ground.

How could he have forgotten?

How could he have let himself slip into this fantasy?

This was not an old-world fairy tale. Where the crows ate your eyes, ships were dashed on the rocks and the dark magic won. This was not happy endings and true love.

Those things did not exist.

"I am the King. I am not... I'm not your boyfriend. We are not on a date. I forgot, for a moment, who I am and what I must do. But I will not forget again. My word is law, Tinley. We will marry next week. You will take your place as my Queen. You will do your duty. And that is all."

He marched her into the palace, up to her room. "Put the cat away."

Then he went furiously to his own chamber, slamming the door behind him and pacing the length of it.

He had forgotten himself. He had forgotten himself again. It was unforgivable.

And the exact same thing had nearly happened.

He had nearly lost her. Because of his own selfishness. Because he had taken his eyes off of his duty. And he had given in to temptation. It could not be endured. It could not be.

And it never would be. Never again. He was not a man, he was a king. And he would not forget.

It was only two days till the wedding. Alex had not come to her bed, and she had endured endless days of frost ever since she had gone into the wood. She knew what he was doing. It was all related to those things he'd said to her about not being able to be a man and a king. Not being able to have fun. To ever loosen the hold on his reins.

Because if he did, bad things would happen. And somehow, the picnic, all of that, had combined to create the perfect storm inside of him the other day.

She'd been so stupid going into the wood. She knew she had been. But she had been…

It was difficult to explain the journey she was on

in herself, and it was not terribly compatible with the journey he was on.

But she was finding courage. Finding her own feet, and it made him want to lock down and control her.

There had to be a middle ground. Had to be something else. Had to be a path to freedom.

For both of them.

She made sure the animals were fed and happy, Algernon sleeping on the bed, the others in their habitats, and she decided that she was going to do something to breach the silence between them.

She walked down the hall, toward his bedroom. She had always let him determine when they might sleep together, but she was done with that.

She wasn't afraid to put herself forward. Wasn't afraid of being rejected.

She didn't know why.

Because you know now it has nothing to do with you, even if he does tell you to leave.

It was true. She did know that. And she knew it well. She had found a sort of comfort with herself here, in a place she would have said should've made her the most uncomfortable.

And it was magic.

She felt magic, even now in this precarious position. She slipped down the hallway and she paused in front of that family portrait she had looked at when she had first arrived.

Her eye went right to Alexius.

And she didn't feel lonely. She didn't feel isolated.

No, he wasn't quite where she wanted him to be. And she didn't know how long it would take for him to get there.

But he was… He was hers.

And she had found a way to open herself up, join all of the pieces together. No longer compartmentalized.

He understood her. Understood the life she had here at the palace, and he had gotten to know the person that time spent in Boston at school had helped shape her into.

He understood about the charity, and he tolerated her animals.

He knew her in a way that nobody else ever had. Perhaps in a way no one else ever would.

And it made her chest burn bright.

She'd made a mistake. Going into the wood had been a mistake, but she had a feeling it was one she had to make.

Without knocking, she pushed open the door to his bedroom. And there he was, lying on the bed, that lounging predator. His eyes were sharp, hard. "What are you doing here, Tinley?"

"I think it's past time we talked, don't you?"

"Why would you say that?"

"Well, because. Because we ought to, don't you think? About what happened."

"I wasn't confused about the incident that you might want to speak about."

"Good," she said. "I'm glad that you weren't confused. Because it's important. It's important that we have this discussion. I… I'm very sorry. I didn't think. I didn't think, and I should have. It was so important to me to go get Algie that I didn't think about my own safety. But I want you to know that I would've crashed in even if you were standing out there. You would have had to come after me either way."

"I would have stopped you."

"It doesn't matter. It doesn't change the fact that I would have needed to go in after him."

"I would've gone for you."

"All right. But you can't control me, Alex. I'm finding myself for the first time in my life, and I don't want to be married to a man who wants to control my every breath. That's a thing. I really don't want a king. I want you. And I know that you think they're one and the same, but they aren't. I belong to you. But you do not rule me."

"They're the same."

"They aren't. Because a king is born ruling over a people, royalty is inevitable. But love? I give you that. Freely."

"Love?" he asked, his voice deadly.

"Yes," she said. "Love. I… I love you, Alexius."

His eyes were flat, his chest pitching with the effort it took him to draw in breath. He looked angry. More than angry. He looked furious. This was the first time she had ever truly feared him.

"Love is not what a sane person would call this thing between us."

"Perhaps I'm not sane, then. It wouldn't surprise me overly much."

"Love is a distraction. Love is a lie."

"It feels very much like the truth to me."

"Yes, it was the truth to you when you thought you loved Dionysus as well. When are you going to accept that your naivety makes you believe things that simply aren't true?"

"You don't get to tell me what it is I feel. You don't get to tell me who I am or what I'm naïve about. I might have been wrong about Dionysus, but that doesn't mean I'm wrong about you. I'm not. I understand what this is between us. It's real. You cannot tell me otherwise."

"No," he said. "I trust my head. I do not trust my heart."

"Because of Lazarus? You were a boy, Alex, and you were forced to pay for sins that not even a man should have to pay for. Accidents happen."

"One time is an accident," he said. "Twice is not."

"It isn't the same. I understand why it feels that way, but it isn't. It isn't, and it never could be. Dionysus was responsible for his own actions, as a man. He might've been young, but he was still an adult man. What happened to Lazarus is a tragedy, what happened to Dionysus is… Idiocy. An idiocy that was not yours."

"No," he said, his voice harsh. "There is something you don't know."

"There's nothing you could tell me that would make me change the way that I feel."

"The night that Dionysus went into the wood I did not discourage him. In fact, I was glad of it."

"What?"

"I knew he was going to create a spectacle. Dragging that socialite who was with him off into the darkness. I knew it would create a sensation, and that you would know for certain what he'd been up to that night. And in fact, I was coming to tell you."

"You… You were?"

"Yes. I was intent on letting you know just how unsuitable your fiancé really was. That even now, so close to when the two of you were to be married, he was off with another woman, all showing off and being a fool. And I was going to seduce you."

"What?"

"Oh, yes," he said. "You see, I wanted you for myself. And as long as I thought my brother was keeping his vows to you, I wasn't going to touch you. But then he didn't. He didn't, and I thought that you deserved to know. And that I would make you mine. But Tinley, I was not going to offer you marriage. I was going to offer you the chance to be my mistress. Such is my weakness. I was going to take advantage of the fact that my brother was drunk, that he was a fool, and use it to maneuver myself into a situation where I might have his fiancée. His future Princess. I felt we could come to an arrangement that would be quite satisfactory to us both."

"But you… You didn't come to me."

"I was on my way, when I got the news of my brother's death. I let my brother go into the woods so that I could seduce his fiancée. There is no sugarcoating that. I let my first brother die because I wanted to go off and have fun. I let my second brother die for the same reason. Do you not see? I am selfish. I am weak. More than either of them could ever be. Though, they're dead. So it makes no difference, does it?"

"Alex…"

Shock slammed through her. She tried to imagine the self that she'd been then. Young and fragile. Naïve.

What would have happened if she'd found out before his death that Dionysus had gone off with another woman, even while she was in the palace? Feeling like she loved him? And what would she have done to the bearer of the news? And if he tried to seduce her?

She had thought then that she'd hated Alex. But she recognized now that the intensity of emotion she felt in his presence was desire, and not hatred.

She had rejected it at the time because she had been young. But… But if he had kissed her? If he had offered her comfort in her moment of being made a fool of, would she have given him her virginity even then? And what would he have thought then? Discovering that she had never been with his brother?

And she waited. She waited to feel something. To feel disgust. To feel angry with him for that. For allowing that low moment to occur, so that he could try to take advantage of it, except all she felt was…

A sense of regret.

For it was possible that she could have been with Alex even then.

Yes, and you would've felt guilt forever. If you'd been sleeping with Alex while Dionysus was being attacked.

It was true. Any resentment that she felt toward Alex all these years… It would've been worse, would've been magnified had the things between them come to a head then.

And she'd…she'd needed those years away.

She'd needed to spend time on her own. To learn things, and find things out about herself.

For the woman she was now with Alex was not the woman she'd been then. Eighteen and full of doubt in regard to herself.

No, she hadn't been the same woman then at all.

She'd truly been a girl. And not ready for any of the situations she'd found herself in.

But she had become more. She had become stronger and better since.

And she knew Alex had too.

"Alex, no matter what… It was still his choice. It was still…"

"It was my weakness. My selfishness. And then, that same weakness nearly got you killed as well. For I do not know who I am when I'm around you. I do not know…

"I thought that I could turn you into a duty, and I thought that I could fix this. I thought you were more dangerous wandering around in the world belonging to another man than you ever could have been as my Queen. But I underestimate the power of this curse on my family. I underestimate the power of my own weakness."

"Look at me," she said, poking her own chest. "I am not eaten by wolves. I'm here. In front of you. I am the woman that you wanted then, but I'm stronger now. I'm choosing to stand here. Whatever you might think. I choose to be with you. We are stronger than this. What happened all those years ago was a tragedy. And I wish... I only wish that if we could have been together then, we were able to be strong enough to recognize the feelings we had. But I wasn't. I was young, and I was immature. And I couldn't figure out what I wanted. I was happy to go along pleasing my father because I could get no approval from my mother. I felt resentment toward you because you were the brother my mom wanted me to be with. And because you made me feel things I wasn't ready to feel. I wouldn't have been ready for your seduction then. It would've burnt me alive."

She blinked furiously. "And you... You were still punishing yourself. And you still are. But it has to stop. We are more than this. We can be more. I love you. And it doesn't matter what happened then. It doesn't matter who my father thought I should be with, who your father thought you should be with. It doesn't matter that my mother wants me to be Queen. I don't care about being Queen. But I do care about being your wife. I love you, Alexius. King and man, it makes no difference to me, but you have to understand I would take you gladly without the title of King. But I could never take a king that wasn't you. So in the end, it's not all the same. It is the man that matters. For it is the man that makes a difference. It is the man I want. It is the man I need. And I don't care that you think you were weak. I find you to be strong."

"You don't care about the truth? You don't care about lies? That's all this is. Pretty lies you're telling yourself to make it all feel okay. Because you're drunk on sex and desire, and you don't understand the difference between that and love."

"No. You don't understand the difference between a curse and life. You don't understand the difference between a king and a martyr. You want to blame yourself for all of this, and for the life of me I can't understand why. Why is it so important to you that all of this is your fault?"

"Enough," he said, his voice hard. "If you wish to be my Queen, come here and demonstrate your supplication."

It was so clear what he was doing. What he had always done. This thing between them was so intense, so undeniable that he wanted distance. He'd done it by disapproving. He did it now with cruelty. But she could see him. She could see what he was doing. "Is that what you want? You want to degrade me?"

She took a step toward him, her heart thundering in her chest. "You can't."

He reached out and curved his hand around her throat, urging her toward him. The dominant hold sent a shock of desire, of excitement and trepidation through her. "I can degrade you. You have only seen a taste of my destruction, Tinley."

"The only person you're destroying is yourself. And you cannot degrade me if I choose everything that happens between us here." She dropped to her knees. "It's my choice. Does that make it degradation or worship?" She reached up, undoing his slacks, and freeing his manhood. She squeezed him tight, running her hand up and down his hard length. "Am I to feel degraded now?"

She looked up at him, at the torment on his face. "I think it's you who feels shame. I don't feel shame. I love you. And this thing between us could never feel wrong. Not to me."

He reached out and wrapped his fingers around her hair. "What do you know? You've gone from hating me to wanting me to loving me in the space of weeks. How will it change, then, tomorrow?"

"It won't."

"It will," he growled. "It will, because it inevitably does. I will fail you in some regard and lose your good favor. And once it's gone, it will be gone forever. Mistakes change you. And they change how you are seen. No one loves unconditionally."

"My feelings haven't changed. But I have. And I recognize now what burned within me all those years ago. But I couldn't have you, Alex. What was the point of feeling these things? What was the point when I could never have you? And so they sat inside of me, fuzzy and half realized, and nothing quite like what they are now."

"Do not test me."

But she did. She leaned forward and flicked her tongue over his heated length, desire gathering at the base of her spine. She loved him. Every inch of him. Strong and hard and masculine. Glorious. He was everything that she could ever want. Everything she could ever hope for. He was a man. Tortured, alone in a hell of his own making.

His own making? Somebody put him here.

It was true. And she recognized the truth of that as soon as she had the thought. As soon as it entered her head.

His hell had been created by someone. By Dionysus? Who had told him all these things? Who had given him love once and then taken it away?

And so she set about showing him that she never would. She took him deeply into her mouth, luxuriating in him. In all that he was. And all the two of them created together. The heat and the fire. The need too.

There was something blessed about needing another person like this. Something glorious and outrageous, and far beyond anything she had ever hoped to experience before.

It was a relief, actually. To need.

She couldn't explain it. Except that it made her feel more connected, more, than she ever had before. Except that it created in her a deep sense of purpose and desire.

It made her feel important. It was that belonging, and being belonged to.

That singular relationship she had found with him.

Fate, maybe.

Except… If they had always been fated, they might have found each other earlier. But even fate required a choice.

And she was grateful for the choice.

Grateful for the power that she found within it.

He was shaking beneath her, trembling with need. And oh, how she loved it. She pushed them both to the edge, until he growled and hauled her to her feet. "Enough. Undress me."

She removed the rest of his clothes, leaving him a glorious, naked warrior before her. A man carved from stone, but a man all the same.

He wanted her. And he might hate himself for it, but he could not be icy when they were together like this. It was impossible.

For in this, there was power. Real power. And maybe here, she would be able to show him that she wasn't lying. That her love was unconditional. But there wasn't a horrible story about mistakes he made that he could tell her that would have her turning against him.

No.

He kissed her. Fierce and hard, with everything he had.

And she thought, for a moment, for a glimmer, that he might know. That he might feel it. He stripped her clothes from her body, his movements forceful, intense. And when she was naked before him, she opened her arms to receive him, and found herself being turned over onto her stomach.

"You say you want a man," he said. "But there is no man. King or beast. That's all there is. You may have the beast, since you seem so eager to test me."

He urged her up onto her knees, and she felt his hardness pressing up against the slick entrance to her body.

"Alex…"

And then he was inside of her, deep and rough, and she cried out, half agony, half ecstasy.

He gripped the back of her neck with one hand, and held her hip fast with the other as he poured his fury, his rage into her body.

He was trying to take their connection and twist it. Trying to turn it into something it wasn't. Trying to make them something they weren't.

She knew because for some reason it was important to him that this be a sin. That this be a failure.

Not a desire. Not love.

It was so important to him that this be a mistake, that she not love him, that he not love her.

He was determined to villainize himself, to weaponize this thing against himself.

And she could not understand why.

The reason was just out of her reach, and as pleasure built inside of her—in spite of the fact that this was rough and dizzying—the answer moved further out of reach.

She couldn't think when he was like this.

She could only feel.

That's the answer. Feeling.

He was thinking. He was doing mental gymnastics to come up with ways to explain away all that they were, but that wasn't right. It wasn't it. It wasn't them.

And so she closed off her mind, and she opened up her heart. A feeling.

"Alex," she whispered, his name on her lips the only sound in the room beyond the harsh slap of their skin as he pounded into her like an animal.

But it wasn't an animal. And he wasn't a beast. Just like all those disparate pieces of her needed to come together, so did his.

He wasn't a man. He wasn't a king. He wasn't the beast.

He was all of them. All at once.

He was desperate and sad and lonely and powerful and weak and vulnerable and dangerous, all at once.

He was everything.

Her world. Her potential destruction.

And it was all so much, so deep, so real and raw that of course he was desperate to turn away from it, because this could be their undoing.

But it could also be their making.

She was certainly determined to have it be hers.

"I love you," she whispered.

He growled and slammed into her one last time, and it sent her over the edge, sparks bursting behind her eyelids. "I love you," she said again. "I love you."

"Stop," he growled.

"I love you," she said. "Why does it scare you so damn much?"

"You cannot love me," he snarled. "I am unlovable."

"You're not."

"My own mother didn't love me, Tinley, you can't. She loved her little boy that wasn't going to be King. The one she could have. The one who belonged to her. Not me. I belong to this country. To my father. She would not hold me at Lazarus's funeral, so little was I her child. I'm not a man. I cannot be. I cannot be yours."

"Alex…"

"The wedding is off."

"What are you saying?"

"The wedding must be called off. This cannot happen. It cannot be."

"Alex, it's too late to call it off. You said so yourself. Everyone is coming. My mother is coming…"

"And that matters to you so very much? I thought it didn't. I thought that you didn't care what she wanted."

"I don't," she said, desperation making her words flow out wrong. Desperation making her clumsy. "That isn't what I meant at all."

And she lay there looking at him, realizing that there was a gulf between them they would not be able to cross unless he chose to. Realizing that he didn't trust her. And if he didn't trust her, there was nothing that could be done.

It isn't you he doesn't trust. It's himself.

Her heart squeezed tight. Burned inside of her chest.

"Alexius…"

"Dionysus was her new pride and joy. She didn't let him near me at all while he was growing up. She didn't trust me with her new son. How could she? I let Lazarus die."

"You didn't," she said, tears starting to fall down her face. Because she knew that whatever she said, it didn't matter. Because his mother had told him these things were true. His mother.

Her own mother had told her that she wasn't good enough. She had believed it. She had believed it because it was so easy. Because the person who taught you to speak, taught you to walk, taught you all those important things, taught you how to feel about yourself. And he was no different. King or not.

"She would rather I had died," he said.

"She would never say that to you," Tinley said, horror rising up in her breast.

"She did," Alex said. "She did. She wished so much that it were me. Lazarus would've been a better king anyway."

"You were a boy," she said.

"It doesn't matter. A boy in my position is never just a boy."

"Sometimes the world is just cruel. And we need something to blame so that we feel like we can control it. We need a villain. Your mother made you a villain. But you were just a child. You are not responsible for this. You're not."

"It doesn't matter. That's what she believed."

"So make a new story. About who you are. About who you can be. It's not too late for that. It's not."

"You are a sweet girl. And you see the world in a rosy sort of way. You care about too many things. Small things. But it makes you blind to the big truth that is right in front of you. I cannot love you, and even if I could, it would only mean destruction for you."

"No," she said.

"It's true, Tinley. You must be reasonable. About this. About us."

"Alex…"

"I will give you all the money you need to care for your charity. I will give you a platform. But you will not be Queen. We will not marry."

"But I want to marry you. Are you so perverse that now that I want it, you don't want to give it to me?"

"It is not about want. It is about what must be done. And about what I must be. You can tell me all you want what you believe to be true, but I've seen the opposite to be so. It isn't just general weakness. You are my weakness. And it cannot be."

"Alex…"

"Get out." He was a raw, wounded animal, his words shredded, his eyes haunted. And they hurt her, his words. But they were designed to. He wanted to hurt her, as he was hurt. Hurt her so she would run.

Knowing it didn't make it hurt less.

"You can't possibly be sending me away."

"I am. Because I must."

"You don't have to do anything. You can make a new choice. You can start over. Your mother is dead. She doesn't get to decide who you are."

"My brothers are also dead. And they can never decide who they want to be. And that's because of me."

"This is only impossible because you're making it impossible."

"If that's how you have to see it, then that is the way of it. I am the King. And if I choose for it to be impossible, then it will be impossible."

"Don't do this."

"It is done," he said. "And we cannot go back."

Despair broke inside of her like a dam. And instead of following orders, she dropped to her knees.

And she knew that she should be ashamed. Except... She wasn't. She felt brave, even as she was falling apart. She felt powerful. Because she wasn't scared to love in this capacity. With this depth that created despair in her that seemed to block out any and all hope.

He was, though. He was afraid of letting go of the past. He was afraid of what it would mean if he let himself love. He was lost in the middle of the Dark Wood, not her. He had never come back out the day he had gone to search for his brother.

"You have to choose to be found," she said softly. "Nobody can do it for you, Alex. You have to choose."

"I've made my choice."

A broken sob escaped her lips. "Very well," she said. "If this is what you want, I can't make you do anything else. I'm not a king. I'm just a girl who loves you. But think of all the things you have dominion over. Think of all the things you can buy, all the things you can control, and ask yourself if I'm one of them. You could not force this. You could not buy it. I had to choose it. And you have to choose it back. There is no fate. The only person keeping you from being happy right now is you. You can choose to be as good as you want to be. As happy as you want. As miserable as you want. You can choose to be defined by what happened. Or you can choose to move forward. It's up to you. You know where to find me."

She dressed slowly, then walked down the hall. She looked around her room, at the pieces of herself she had brought to the palace. Baskets of yarn stacked in front of ancient tapestries. A cat carrier on an antique highboy. A ferret and two hedgehogs in cages adjacent to an Oriental rug that was probably older than the Ottoman Empire.

And she smiled. In spite of the jagged pieces inside of her heart. She smiled because…she was good enough to be here. And she loved him enough. But she couldn't be healed for him. He had to heal himself. She had chosen to be happy. She had chosen to move on.

To decide that what her mother had told her about herself wasn't true.

And he would have to do the same. In his own time.

As for her part… She would leave. She would leave without taking his money. Because she would find a way. She would.

And she didn't want to use the King. Not at all.

Because she refused to contribute to the story that he told himself about what made him matter.

She could survive on her own. And no matter that she didn't want to, she could.

Without her mother's approval, without inheritance.

Without Alex, even, if it came down to it.

Because loving him had given her something that his rejection could never take away.

She had found herself.

And she had the hope that when he found a way to bring all those pieces of himself together, he would be brave enough to love too.

The gift that she would take away from this palace was that she was enough on her own.

And it allowed her to close the door on a lifetime of pain heaped on her by her mother.

And as she exited her room, and closed the door on this beautiful moment of her life, she knew that she would be taking with her more than she was leaving behind. Lessons and strength and powerful new truths about who she was.

It was just…that the difficult thing was, she was leaving behind one thing that was quite important.

Her heart.

And she didn't know if she would ever have a hope of getting it back.

CHAPTER THIRTEEN

HE HADN'T HAD to check to know that she was gone. He had felt it. Had felt the absence of her as sure as he had ever felt the presence of her. She was gone, and it was a good thing. She was gone, and it was absolutely what he needed. What she needed.

Is it?

He thought that he'd banished pain from his chest as a boy.

For the loss of his brother had been great, severe and intense and it had torn at his tender, untried feelings. But more than that, the rejection his mother had given him after...

When Lazarus had died, he had been a boy mourning his brother. Above all else. And his mother had not held him. Had not comforted him.

You did this.

He could still hear those three words. Could see himself standing there with his arms outstretched and then she'd said that.

He'd needed her.

She'd turned her pain onto him like a knife.

He had learned then, what it meant to be a man. To take blame. To have to soldier on even with that blame resting on your shoulders.

You were a boy.

Yes, he had been a boy. But the end result was the same, whether he was boy or man, so he supposed it didn't matter.

He was the King, and he had to be King. He couldn't... *I love you.*

He could not accept her love. Any more than he could allow her to give it. It would be the end of them both...

Would it? Or are you simply unable to put the ghosts of the past to rest? Just as she said?

No, if she could love him then perhaps these dreadful and terrible things out in the world weren't his fault.

He looked out the window of his bedchamber. He looked down to the wood below.

That was it. It was the site of everything. The place of all his destruction. There were no answers up here, but perhaps...

He tore down the stairs, and out of the palace. He was not drunk, no matter how he had wanted to make the pain go away with drink.

He didn't allow himself such luxuries.

No, he was in his right mind. Utterly and completely sober.

Lazarus had been lost in the wood.

Dionysus.

His fear over Tinley, which had caused him to

realize he was edging too close to his greatest fear, had happened because of the wood.

If it was magic, then it was a dark magic, and it wasn't going away. No matter how much he wanted it to. No matter how much he tried.

If there were answers, they would be there.

Through the darkness, through the mist, Alexius de Prospero, the Lion, charged into the wood.

Alex looked around at the eerie stillness in the trees. There was no sound. Not tonight.

Not even the wolves.

He didn't know what had called him into the forest tonight, but he trusted it.

Which was an odd thing to feel. To think.

For nothing the forest had ever done was particularly trustworthy.

But he was tied to it. Connected in a way he could not escape. And so he moved forward. Until he was back in that same clearing where he found Tinley and the cat. He heard a sound coming from the bushes, and he turned. But it was not a wolf standing there. It was a man.

Tall, his features obscured by shadow.

"State your business," Alex said.

"Do I need official business to speak to my brother?"

She had gone to her mother's house in Rome. She knew it was a strange choice, considering she was raw and vulnerable and it would be easy enough for her mother to take strips off her in her current state.

Except… That would have been true if Tinley had been unchanged by her time with Alex.

But she had been. Utterly and completely.

Walking into her mother's drawing room, her inner sanctum, made Tinley's chest go tight, but she didn't feel nervous. She didn't feel cowed or afraid.

Her mother was lounging on a chaise, her red hair more a dark copper, sleek and twisted up into an elegant chignon. "Tinley," she said. "I'm quite surprised to see you here."

"Why is that? I am your daughter."

"You haven't been here for the past four years. Why would you show your face now? Especially in light of your broken engagement to King Alexius. It is being talked about in all of the important social circles. Soon to be in the news, I suspect. Though, I must admit, the dissolution of the arrangement surprises me less than the arrangement itself."

"How wonderfully predictable for you, then," Tinley said.

And if she meant that it was predictable her mother had said such a thing, and not that the turn of events was predictable, it was open to interpretation.

"Well," she said. "What will you do now?"

"I don't know. I'll continue to work with my charity. I'm going to be putting on more events. Speaking more."

"It's quite fashionable to be involved in charities, Tinley, but not really in the way you do it."

"I don't care about being fashionable."

Her mother's brows rose a fraction. "Oh?"

"Why does that surprise you? I've never done anything to indicate that I cared about being in fashion."

"I assume that you couldn't," her mother said, "not that you wouldn't."

It was a strange thing, because her mother was being hurtful, that was undeniable. But she was also being…genuine. And suddenly Tinley saw things through an entirely different lens. Her mother truly believed these things. That Tinley would be happier only if she found favor with the fashionable people. That she would be happier with a certain measure of status. That she would be happier if her hair was straight or her freckles faded.

"We don't want the same things," Tinley said. "I want… I want to make a difference. And I want to spend less than five minutes on my hair in the morning. I want to find a man who loves me." It made her chest catch to say it. "Who loves me as much as I love him. And I don't care if he's a king. A prince. A pauper. It doesn't matter. I just want someone to love me. With my five-minute hair and my unfashionable charitable pursuits. With my cat and my other animals. I just want to be me. I'm… I'm happy with myself."

"That's impossible," her mother said. "Nobody's happy with themselves."

Tinley's heart crumpled. "I… You believe that, don't you?"

"The public is never entirely happy with anything

I do," her mother said. "How can I be happy with it, then?"

"There's always room for improving yourself, mom, and I don't mean looks. I mean your heart. What does it matter if your hair sits just right if the content of who you are is all wrong? That's what I work at. It's what I'm trying to find my way with. I want to be happy with the person I am in my heart. The rest of it doesn't much matter."

"The press doesn't care about your heart."

"And I don't care about the press. So it's all fine then."

"Tinley…"

"I love him," Tinley said. "I hope you know that. I'm actually heartbroken. Because I was in love with Alex. I've been in love with him for a long time. But I didn't care about being his Queen. That was why I was there. It was why I was with him."

"Love? Darling, in the grand scheme of all the years you will be joined to a man, love doesn't mean much of anything. You need to want the life that he can bring you."

"Things, Mum, you're talking about things. I don't care about things. I care about…" She imagined then, the way that he had lain on top of her in the grass. The way that he had come for her in the wood. How beautiful he found her in sweats or a ball gown. "It's not in the house you live in. It's in the small things between you."

"Small things won't keep you fed. I married a man

with influence, in hopes that my child might have influence. Might have better."

"I do have better. It's just not the better you wished I wanted." She let that truth settle between them.

Staring at her mother now, she realized that it had been easy for her to make one parent a saint, and the other a villain. Her mother had hurt her, yes. But her father had not been a perfect man. He had controlled her life. Had wanted a very particular thing for her as well.

It was just he had known how to work with Tinley rather than against her to accomplish it. But even from beyond the grave he had dictated she marry and when.

He had not been a good husband to her mother. He had been distant, had taken Tinley to live at the palace part time.

He had allowed there to be distance in his marriage and all that blame could not fall on her mother.

For it took two people to be in a marriage, to be in a relationship, and now that she truly loved someone she could see that.

"I understand love. And I won't marry for anything less than that. I want better than the quiet, strained household that you and dad made. And now that I'm older, I can understand that it wasn't only your fault. For he was in that marriage too. And whatever he did to make you think… To make you think the most important thing between you was his status, he has fault in that. But I want better than that. And I found it. Even though things have fallen apart now, I know who I am. I know what I want."

"Wanting something you can't have isn't better," her mother said, and in that partially spoken statement was a wealth of truth.

Wanting a love her mother *couldn't* have. So her mother had wanted *things*, because her marriage could not give her real love, real deep emotional satisfaction.

"You can want it now," Tinley said. "You could find love now."

"Well. You aren't going to find it with your hair looking like that."

She watched her mother close in on herself. Hide because she was… She was afraid.

In that moment, Tinley saw that if her mother admitted that Tinley was right, she'd have to admit she'd made mistakes when her daughter was young. And she couldn't do it. Not now.

And Tinley wasn't…wounded or angry or any of the things that she expected to be. Because she was too confident in the position she stood in now. Too confident in what she had been fashioned into.

Because of Alex.

And she felt bruised with not having him.

But not broken.

For she was able to stand before her mother now, and feel confident. Feel no shame. And see the wound in her mother, rather than just seeing her own.

"I will come to visit again," Tinley said. "But I

hope… I hope things change for you between now and then."

And she walked out of her mother's house with her head held high, and a certain measure of confidence in her heart.

Her life might not look exactly how she wanted it to. But she had become the woman she needed to be.

And she would have to be able to find some solace in that.

CHAPTER FOURTEEN

THE MAN STEPPED into the light, a pale beam cast there by the moon. Alex stared at this man, but he could not recognize him. Half of his face was scarred. He was as tall as Alex, but broader, his body that of a warrior's.

"Who are you?"

"It really spoils the theater that you haven't guessed yet. But who do you think? Mother named me to enable coming back from the dead in a rather dramatic fashion. Though she could never have planned such intense irony. Honestly I've been waiting for the reveal for a very long time."

"Lazarus."

"Yes."

"How?" It was the only question he could ask, because there were so many, and they were all trapped in his throat.

"That isn't the interesting part. Not really. Because the how is easy. Your assumption was that something killed me in the wood. That was the assumption of everyone. But I was taken. Not murdered. Though I suppose," he spread his arms wide, "the fact I wasn't murdered is fairly self-evident at this point."

"What are you doing here now?"

"Oh, I came to take your bride."

He said it with the casual arrogance that only Alex ever spoke with. Certain no one ever spoke that way to him.

"Why?"

"Revenge."

"Against me?"

"Yes. I… I hate this place," he said, looking around the wood. "Not the forest. I hate this country. And for years I've hated you most of all. I can't say you're my favorite person now."

"We were children," Alex said. "It devastated Mother that you were gone. It nearly destroyed Father."

"And you?"

"I couldn't let it destroy me. I had to be the King."

"That is the thing," Lazarus said. "I think you did let it destroy you. It's why I didn't take her."

"Who?"

"Your little fiancée. I was watching you both from the wood. It was easy enough to lure her cat into the trees, and once the cat was here, she followed. Predictable. I was going to kidnap her. But I realized something. In this dispute between the two of us, she's…innocent."

His brother seemed perplexed by the idea that Tinley's innocence had affected him.

"She is," Alex agreed. "And if you had put a hand on her… I would like for you to remain back from the dead, Lazarus, I would hate to send you back to the grave. And if you put a hand on her…"

"I thought as much," Lazarus said. "Though that is not what stopped me. The way she looked at you… She loves you. Alex, I was taken into a society of people who despised me. Love is a rare commodity in the world. Love like she feels for you."

"What does her loving me have to do with anything?" The very question made a streak of pain tear through his chest.

"Because the way that I was brought up, Alex, there is little but hate in my heart for anyone or anything. I was created to come back and destroy you. But my captor died. And…" His brother looked into the distance. "I don't care. I don't want to be a pawn. Not of the crown of Liri, and not against her detractors. There are truths about our family that would be difficult for you to stomach, I've a feeling. Truths that go back further than Father. All those wars we fought for all those years, all those mysterious deaths in the wood. Why do you think people are kept out of here? It's not the wolves."

"It's not…"

"There are people here. Oppressed by this country. I was taken to be a symbol."

"But you weren't used."

"Things didn't go as planned. The woman Dionysus was with that night… She lured him into the wood. It was never wolves."

"Is he…"

"He's dead. I was not a part of that. You must believe it. And that, is where my fault lies. I cannot bring myself to kill you. Any more than I could've brought myself to kill him. Just as I couldn't take your woman. She loves you. And you love her. Those are gifts that I will never have, Brother, for they were stripped away from me a long time ago. And I let that fester into hatred, of you, of this place. Which was exactly what my captors wanted. But I… I see a different path."

"What path? I don't understand."

"You might be the Lion of the Dark Wood, but I am the Prince. And I have my own people to protect. And you and I… Well, we have some negotiating to do."

"Surely that can wait."

"It can. Though… I heard that you broke your engagement."

"Yes. I did."

"Why? As I said, it was clear to me there was a great deal of love between the two of you. You don't have to stand in front of a fire to know it's warm. I don't have to be able to feel love to be able to recognize it."

"You might have been raised to hate me, Lazarus, but you… You cannot possibly hate me more than I was trained to hate myself."

"And is that why you can't be with her?"

"She doesn't deserve to be tied to someone like me."

"She doesn't deserve to be with a man she's clearly in love with?"

"It is not so simple."

"Life is actually quite simple," Lazarus said. "You must live. Whatever it is that's in front of you, take it if you can. For there are guarantees of nothing. I was born a prince in a castle, ended up raised in a shack in the woods. If you can have the castle, why are you choosing the shack?"

"What does that have to…"

"You can have love, you're choosing not to. Don't be a fool. You and I will have a meeting in a few days. But I expect you will have resolved things with your Queen by then."

And just as quietly and suddenly as he had appeared, Lazarus was gone. And everything Alex thought he knew about the world had been turned on its head.

Lazarus made it sound like a choice.

Lazarus was alive.

He was *alive*.

And if he was alive… If there was more to all of this than Alex had ever known…

But perhaps he didn't know everything.

Perhaps it didn't have to be the end of him and Tinley. Because they had something that had stopped Lazarus from taking revenge.

Something powerful.

And he… He was choosing fear instead.

He had hidden behind the title, because it meant

he didn't have to feel. Not the grief over losing either of his brothers, or the pain of his mother's rejection.

But Tinley had asked for the man.

And suddenly, he realized, there wasn't only death in the wood, there was life too. And life was much the same. There wasn't only death. He wasn't only the King. There were miracles, and there were tragedies. There was pain and there was joy. There was hate, but there was love.

And as with Lazarus, love had won over hate.

Love had won.

He wished…very much that his mother had lived to see this. She had been hopeless, that was the problem. She had been hopeless and had seen no other way. And he… It had pushed him into that place too.

But there was hope.

There was life.

He no longer needed to carry the hurt his mother had put there. The sad thing was her life had ended before she could put it aside. But he could choose to. Now. He could choose hope.

He could choose love.

He needed Tinley.

Immediately.

Tinley was working on a sweater for her cat.

She felt that she had descended to some new low, but at the same time, it was so cute it felt like it could be a high. Life was funny.

She brought her needle around to the front of the yarn for a purl, when there was a knock on her cottage door. She shoved the work back onto the needles and set it down. "Yes?"

She wasn't expecting anyone, and it wasn't like her cottage was in the sort of place that got a lot of foot traffic. She stood up and peered out one lace curtain, and then her heart scurried up into her throat.

"Alex?" she called.

"Let me in," he said.

"I'll… All right."

She went and jerked the door open, and there he was, tall and broad as ever. But disheveled. He looked tired, as if he hadn't been sleeping.

Join the club.

"What are you doing here?"

"I have so much to tell you," he said. "The first of which is that Lazarus is alive."

"What?"

"He's alive. And… There is more to that story, which I will explain, but first… I was afraid. Because I thought there was no way you could possibly love me. Not when my mother seemed to see how unworthy I was."

"Alex, it's never been about worthiness…"

"I know. I do now. It was easier, though, to accept that. Because it required nothing of me. And I've experienced my share of loss. So it was easier to hide behind the title of King. To hide behind duty. When Dionysus died, when I made the decision to seduce you while he was away for the evening… I was acting with my heart. And over the years, I've dismissed it. As lust. Because it was easier than admitting that those feelings I had for you were complicated. But the timing of everything was complicated, and it wasn't evil of me to want you. Things happened the way they did. I will never be glad that he's gone. Ever. But I do wonder if I would have ever had the courage then to override what everyone wanted because love is stronger. I wonder if I would have been able to admit that I loved you." He moved closer to her, cupped her chin. "It doesn't matter now. What I would have done. What matters is that I'm here now. We cannot change the past. But we have a choice now. I have a choice now. And I choose to make the future the best it can be. I love you, Tinley. I want you to be mine. My wife. My Queen. Marry the man and the King."

"Of course I will," she said, love bursting through her chest like a flame. She wrapped her arms around his neck and kissed him.

"You're my lioness," he said, touching her hair. "How did I not see it before? The signs were everywhere."

"Alex. It's so easy to get caught up in the stories everyone else tells about you. But at some point we have to start telling our own."

"Yes. We must."

"Well, I suppose marriage is really the only course of action."

"I couldn't agree more. It's why I have brought the vicar with me."

"The vicar?" She blinked. "Now?"

"We can have a wedding for the benefit of the

country. But I think we should have one now. For the benefit of us. Only us. This isn't for your mother. It isn't a symbol. It's not because I told my father I would take care of you, it's not because you will be a good queen—though you will. It is simply because I love you. And I will marry you here. With your animals as attendants."

"Really, that is the most ridiculous thing I've ever heard you say."

"I thought you would appreciate it."

"I do. So much."

"So will you marry me? Outside your cottage, on the edge of the wood?"

"I will. And we can have pie as a wedding treat."

"I can think of nothing better."

"I'm very glad we're writing our own story, Alex," she said. "Because I know just how I wanted it to end."

"Do you?"

"Yes. Happily ever after."

EPILOGUE

OF COURSE THEY did have to have a wedding, for the benefit of the nation. Things had changed dramatically in the time since they'd had their private ceremony at the cottage. Tinley had discovered she was expecting the royal heir, a cause for celebration in Liri, but celebrated most of all in the palace, between the King and Queen.

Tinley's mother had fallen in love with an Italian count, and the man was her guest at the wedding.

And Lazarus was in attendance, along with his people. Reconciliation was being worked on, and the true history of Liri over generations was being brought to light. There were some hard truths to that. But Alex was passionate about making things right.

With his brother by his side.

But even more importantly, with his Queen.

When he spoke his vows to her, they came from his heart. The heart that was healing. That no longer felt so scarred.

The heart that had beaten for Tinley Markham

from the very beginning. And he no longer looked back on those feelings as a sin, but a sign.

That love had always been there. And that in the end, love would always prevail.

For love was the source of all magic. Love could overwhelm curses.

Love was a light that no darkness could stand against. And for all his days Alex was committed to choosing love, with Tinley, forever.

* * * * *

Swept up in the magic of
His Majesty's Forbidden Temptation?
You'll be sure to adore these other
Maisey Yates stories!

Crowned for My Royal Baby
Crowning His Convenient Princess
The Queen's Baby Scandal
His Forbidden Pregnant Princess

Available now!

WE HOPE YOU ENJOYED
THIS BOOK FROM
⬧HARLEQUIN
PRESENTS

Escape to exotic locations where passion knows no bounds.

Welcome to the glamorous lives of royals and billionaires, where passion knows no bounds. Be swept into a world of luxury, wealth and exotic locations.

8 NEW BOOKS AVAILABLE EVERY MONTH!

#3877 THE KING'S BRIDE BY ARRANGEMENT
Sovereigns and Scandals
by Annie West

The long-standing betrothal of Princess Eva and King Paul is a political match. He's ready to release her from their promise, until an explosive kiss has him questioning everything he thought he knew about his royal bride!

#3878 THE COMMANDING ITALIAN'S CHALLENGE
by Maya Blake

By-the-book Maceo has fought to protect his company. He won't let free-spirited Faye upend his entire world by claiming it as her inheritance, without proving herself worthy. His challenge? Resisting their chemistry!

#3879 BREAKING THE PLAYBOY'S RULES
Wanted: A Billionaire
by Melanie Milburne

Millie tried to deny the sizzling chemistry with outrageously attractive Hunter before. The pain of her last relationship has made her wary. But when he breaks all his rules to whisk her off to Greece, she can't help that he makes her heart race...

#3880 HOW TO UNDO THE PROUD BILLIONAIRE
South Africa's Scandalous Billionaires
by Joss Wood

Hosting South Africa's wedding of the year is Radd Tempest-Vane's ticket to restoring his family's empire. As long as he finds a new florist, fast! Brinley Riddell is the perfect candidate...but an immediate, dangerous distraction!

YOU CAN FIND MORE INFORMATION ON UPCOMING HARLEQUIN TITLES, FREE EXCERPTS AND MORE AT HARLEQUIN.COM.

HPCNMRB1220

"How was the party?"

Becky had to untie her tongue to speak. "Okay. Everyone looked like they were having fun."

"But not you?"

"No." She sank down onto the wooden step to take the weight off her weary legs and rested her back against a pillar.

"Why not?"

"Because I'm a day late."

She heard him suck in a breath. "Is that normal for you?"

"No." Panic and excitement swelled sharply in equal measure as they did every time she allowed herself to read the signs that were all there. Tender breasts. Fatigue. The ripple of nausea she'd experienced that morning when she'd passed Paula's husband outside and caught a whiff of his cigarette smoke. Excitement that she could have a child growing inside her. Panic at what this meant.

Scared she was going to cry, she scrambled back to her feet. "Let's give it another couple of days. If it hasn't come by then, I'll take a test."

She would have gone inside if Emiliano hadn't leaned forward and gently taken hold of her wrist. "Sit with me."

Opening her mouth to tell him she needed sleep, she stared into his eyes and found herself temporarily mute.

For the first time since they'd conceived—and in her heart she was now certain they had conceived—there was no antipathy in his stare, just a steadfastness that lightened the weight on her shoulders.

Gingerly, she sat beside him, but there was no hope of keeping a distance for Emiliano put his beer bottle down and hooked an arm around her waist to draw her to him.

Much as she wanted to resist, she leaned into him and rested her cheek on his chest.

"Don't be afraid, *bomboncita*," he murmured into the top of her head. "We will get through this together."

Nothing more was said for the longest time and for that she was grateful. Closing her eyes, she was able to take comfort from the strength of his heartbeat against her ear and his hands stroking her back and hair so tenderly. There was something so very solid and real about him, an energy always zipping beneath his skin even in moments of stillness.

He dragged a thumb over her cheek and then rested it under her chin to tilt her face to his. Then, slowly, his face lowered and his lips caught hers in a kiss so tender that the little of her not already melting to be held in his arms turned to fondue.

Feeling as if she'd slipped into a dream, Becky moved her mouth in time with his, a deepening caress that sang to her senses as she inhaled the scent of his breath and the muskiness of his skin. Her fingers tiptoed up his chest, then flattened against his neck. The pulse at the base thumped against the palm of her hand.

But even as every crevice in her body thrilled, a part of her brain refused to switch off, and it was with huge reluctance that she broke the kiss and gently pulled away from him.

"Not a good idea," she said shakily as her body howled in protest.

Emiliano gave a look of such sensuality her pelvis pulsed. "Why?"

Fearing he would reach for her again, she shifted to the other side of the swing chair and patted the space beside her for the dogs to jump up and act as a barrier between them. They failed to oblige. "Aren't we in a big enough mess?"

Eyes not leaving her face, he picked up his beer and took a long drink. "That depends on how you look at it. To me, the likelihood that you're pregnant makes things simple. I want you. You want me. Why fight it anymore when we're going to be bound together?"

Don't miss
The Cost of Claiming His Heir,
available January 2021 wherever
Harlequin Presents books and ebooks are sold.

Harlequin.com

Get 4 FREE REWARDS!

We'll send you 2 FREE Books plus <u>2</u> FREE Mystery Gifts.

Harlequin Presents books feature the glamorous lives of royals and billionaires in a world of exotic locations, where passion knows no bounds.

FREE
Value Over
$20

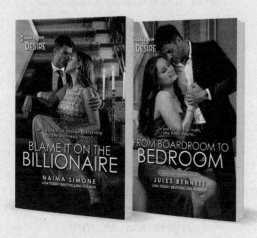

Love Harlequin romance?

DISCOVER.

Be the first to find out about promotions, news and exclusive content!

Facebook.com/HarlequinBooks

Twitter.com/HarlequinBooks

Instagram.com/HarlequinBooks

Pinterest.com/HarlequinBooks

ReaderService.com

EXPLORE.

Sign up for the Harlequin e-newsletter and download a free book from any series at **TryHarlequin.com**

CONNECT.

Join our Harlequin community to share your thoughts and connect with other romance readers!
Facebook.com/groups/HarlequinConnection